SUMMERTIME WITH A CHICAGO THUG

PATRICE BALARK

Twyla T Presents

SUMMERTIME WITH A CHICAGO THUG

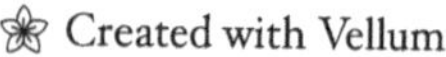 Created with Vellum

MAILING LIST

ARE YOU ON THE LIST?

Click here https://bit.ly/2MO25jK
to join Twyla T. Presents' mailing list and receive new book release
alerts, exclusive giveaways, sneak peeks & more!

Receive instant new book release alerts by texting TwylaT to 22828

RED DIAMOND EDITING BY
V. RENA

reddiamondediting5@yahoo.com

CHICAGO SLANG GLOSSARY

On My Grandma –when someone is trying to prove that they are telling the truth, however, nine times out of ten, they're lying.

Pop - A carbonated soft drink. *WTF is a soda?*

Goofass – a person who says something stupid or does something stupid.

Lord - comes from the Chicago based gang Vice Lords. A friendly termed used nowadays towards ANYONE, specially said by residents of OutWest, Illinois aka *THE BEST PART OF CHICAGO!*

On Foe' Nem (OFN): a termed used by the Four Corner Hustlers (4CH) gang. It's similar to saying, "On my brothers," "On my gang," or "On My Mama."

Merch It – put it on somebody: Reference to "On my Grandma."

Check it out – RUN... RUN FAST AND NEVER CHECK IT OUT.... It's a set up.

Tweakn' – refers to when someone is tripping or bugging.

Mild sauce - A combination of ketchup, hot sauce, and barbecue sauce that is usually served with fried chicken. You'll find it on the menu at places like Harold's Chicken and Uncle Remus Saucy Fried Chicken.

Joe (Jo) – ANYBODY..... Joe can be **ANYBODY**

WELCOME TO CHICAGO!

❀ I ❀

***J**une 20th – First Day of Summer*

"Shaquita. You know a nigga love you, right?" Law said, looking up as he knelt down on one knee, staring at his girlfriend of the past four years.

Rolling her eyes to the back of her head, Shaquita smacked her lips loudly before allowing him to continue.

"Ain't shit in dez streets for a nigga and I'm ready to prove that to you." He paused again, this time going inside his gray Nike jogging pants and pulling out a black velvet box.

Taking a deep breath after the long dramatic pause, Law opened the box, exposing a beautiful three Carat radiant diamond engagement ring with a French-Set Halo diamond band. The ring was breathtaking and although it was the exact one Shaquita told him she wanted, she couldn't accept it.

"NO LAWRENCE. GET THE FUCK UP AND GET OUT MY HOUSE!" Her eyes cut into his and demanded before attempting to walk away.

"Damn Shaq, what the fuck now? You said you wanted to get married and here I am proposing. This a forty-thousand-dollar engagement ring, Lord. What the fuck you mean get up and get out?" he grabbed her by the arm and convicted before she yanked away.

"I don't give a fuck about the cost of that ring Law and although I do wanna get married ..... I wanna do the shit the right way. With a nigga who *knows* how to keep his dick in his pants and ---"

"SHAQ! I DID NOT FUCK THAT BITCH! ON MY GRANDMA GRAVE, DAT HOE LYING." He barked, springing to his feet and chasing behind her.

Shaquita marched through her three- bedroom duplex gathering the rest of Law's belongings, placing them in a black garbage bag. Two days prior, she received screenshots of her man laying in another woman's bed. It was a random bitch who found her page on Instagram and decided to share the news. Reacting to the photo with the heart emoji, Shaq didn't even bother to respond to her; she took the shit directly to her man.

"That was a hotel party and I was rolling off a pill. I had my shirt off cuz it was hot dan' a muthafucker in there. You always taking these bitches word and running with it. You know these hoes jealous. They all wanna be you." Law pleaded his case while following her around the house like a lost puppy.

"BE ME?" Shaquita stopped in her tracks and yelled.

"THEY WANNA BE *ME*?" She turned around screaming this time, charging towards him with a look of death in her eyes.

"They can **have** this shit.... ALL OF IT! You constantly making me look stupid. You constantly giving these bitches reasons to think they got one up on me." Shaq stood in his face and carped.

"Shaq listen...." Law held his hands up trying to plead his case but it was pointless.

"NO.... *YOU* LISTEN!" Her long pointy red stiletto nail landed on the bridge of his nose.

She was sick and tired of Law and his bullshit and although she's never caught him red-handed, she knew for a fact that her nigga wasn't a saint. Lawrence "Law" Bishop, along with his best friend, were leaders of the "JACK BOYZ", a clique known and feared in Chicago for their vicious dealings in the streets. Law was ruthless, rich, and on top of the world and at 25, there was no way he was ready to settle down.

"I am not pressuring you to marry me. I simply want you to ..... STOP CHEATING!" She snarled, muffin' him on the side of his head.

Shaquita continued to move about her place until she gathered the last of all his items. She knew there was way more laying around in the cut but he'll have to get them another time.

"Shaq, this is just as much as my crib as it is yours...You can't put me out this muthafucker, *I* pay the rent...." Law barked as Shaquita more and more ushered him towards the front door.

"Yeah. Yeah. Yeah... Well *my name* is on the lease so legally.... LAW..." She paused, chuckling at her own joke.

"I can do what the fuck I want." Shaquita remarked before reaching around him and opening the front door.

"Aight man.... WAIT!" Law requested in a calmer tone than the one he was using before.

Smacking her lips, Shaquita stopped and shifted her weight to one side, allowing Law to say whatever it was he had to say. More than likely it was nothing but since her door was standing open and her neighbors were nosey, she didn't want to make a scene.

"My Gold Rolex in yo top drawer, I need that." He looked her dead in the eyes and told her, pissing her off even more.

"Nigga, you a Jack Boy, that Rollie don't mean shit to you..... Get the fuck out my house." Shaq spat before pushing him out of the doorway and slamming it shut.

Turning on her heels, Shaquita walked through her house admiring the fancy and expensive décor. Not many 23-years olds from the hood was living the life she was living. Shaq was what people considered, "hood rich," but outside of the Audi 8 and designer bags, there were brains. Graduating with a 4.0 GPA from Loyola University Nursing Program, Shaq worked as a Recovery Room Nurse at Planned Parenthood.

Flickering off the lights in both the kitchen and living room, Shaquita headed to the bedroom but not before stopping in the bathroom first. Reliving herself, Shaq then headed over to the sink to wash her hands. Taking the water and splashing it on her face, she grabbed a clean washcloth to dry it off. Just as she reached for her toothbrush, the sound of her phone ringing halted those plans. Tossing the towel in the sink, Shaq rushed into her bedroom to answer it before the voicemail did. Unsuccessful at that task, she reached the phone only to notice seven missed calls from Law and the most recent one was from her favorite cousin, Monday. Ignoring both of Law's calls and text messages, Shaq facetimed Monday back before flopping down on the bed.

"You sleep?" Monday asked the moment the call connected.

"Nope. Getting ready for bed. What you doing?" Shaquita asked while searching under the covers for the remote control.

"Girl laying here, trying to make myself get up and pack. I hate it here!" Monday whined, causing Shaquita to snicker at her.

"You laughing but I'm for real. I'm thinking about bringing the basic things and shopping for a completely new wardrobe when I get there." She continued and as crazy as it sounded, Monday was serious.

First cousins by blood, Shaquita and Monday were definitely more like sisters at heart. Growing up inseparable until Monday moved away to California when she was eight. Two years apart in age, the cousins still managed to have a close relationship, even miles apart. Shaquita flew out to California at least five times a year while Monday, on the other hand, never visited. Her parents were the strictest of the strict and hardly allowed Monday out of their sight. They sheltered her and despite their biggest fears, she was now twenty-one and officially an adult.

"I can't believe I haven't been home in thirteen years. I don't know why my parents hate Chicago so much, but they just gon' have to stress out together while I'm gone because I'm sure in the hell not going to be thinking about them." Monday disclosed while Shaq listened on in excitement.

Heading into her first year of law school at Stanford University, Monday snagged a summer internship at one of the largest law firms in Chicago, Kirkland and Ellis. Her nearly perfect record and impressive recommendation letters made her the top law school candidate for the position. Both cousins knew that the only way Monday's parents would approve of the visit was if it bettered her future, so the girls made it happen. Lying to them both, Monday told them that she applied for hundreds of internships when in fact, she only applied for one. Shaquita being the brains behind the idea hated the way her aunt and uncle treated her favorite cousin. Monday's father, a Software Development Manager, and her mom, an Anesthesiologist, were wealthy and well off. Living in a mansion in Calabasas, California, they did whatever they could to keep Monday away from the hood but unfortunately, it was embedded in her. Shaquita and Monday talked for another thirty minutes before Law started blowing up her other line.

"You gon' answer that?" Monday quizzed while Shaq acted oblivious.

"No, FUCK LAW and I mean that shit. I put that nigga out and everything and...."

"Byeeeeee Shaquita Dominque Valentine. That nigga ain't going nowhere and neither are you as a matter of fact. I'll end the call so you can pick up for him." Monday giggled, pissing Shaq off.

"You bet not hang up on me Mo' and I'm not playing with you," she threatened her before finishing.

"I'm dead ass serious, listen to me. I been letting this nigga play with me too long and now it's time to get on my bully. You'll be here for the next three months, I'm *SINGLE*, bitch we *FINE,* and everybody know there's nothing like the Chi in the SUMMERTIME!"

$$\maltese \quad 2 \quad \maltese$$

Monday woke up the next morning bright eyed and bushy tailed. In twenty-four hours, she'd be miles away from her overbearing parents and having the time of her life with her favorite person on Earth. When Shaquita came up with the internship idea, Monday ran with it. She had every desire to be an attorney; she simply wanted to enjoy her senior year while doing it. Rolling over and unplugging her phone, Monday read and replied to a few text messages before heading to Facebook. Scrolling her feed, she responded to a few notifications before heading over to Snapchat, where she did the same. Spending the next hour or so in the bed on her phone, Monday finally fought the sheets back and got out. Heading across the spacious bedroom, she entered into her private bathroom, where she started the shower. Taking a sit on the toilet, Mo' handled her business there before retreating to the sink, where she began her hygiene journey. Spending about fifteen minutes alone on her face routine, Monday then brushed her teeth and jumped inside the steamy shower. Doing a full spin under the water, Mo' insured to wet her hair since she'd be washing it. Grabbing all the necessary products, she spent another thirty minutes under water.

Once she was clean and dried off, Monday went into her drawers to find a pair of panties. After sliding those on, she went inside her walk-in closet and pulled out a pair of green Fashion Nova biker shorts and a white Gucci crop top. She knew that with all the activities she had planned, being comfortable was definitely a requirement. Sliding her feet inside a pair of Gucci flip flops, Monday grabbed the fanny pack to match, her keys, and shades before heading downstairs. Stopping off in the kitchen, Mo' immediately regretted doing so when she noticed both parents sitting at the kitchen table drinking coffee.

"Well look who finally decided to wake up." Her mother, Marcia, announced the second their only child turned the corner.

"Good morning." Monday spoke, heading over to the refrigerator.

Before, when she thought her parents weren't home, Mo' planned on making this huge feast but now her appetite had changed. A bottle of water and egg McMuffin from McDonalds didn't sound so bad after all.

"Laura went to get groceries, if you wait, she'll be back to make breakfast." Her father, Dennis, looked up from the newspaper and reported.

"I'm not hungry. I had a big dinner last night." Monday closed the fridge and uttered before turning to face her parents.

Both of them stared at her as if they were staring through her. She knew that they knew she was lying, she just prayed they didn't call her out on it.

"You dressed early, where you going, to the law library?" Marcia smirked before taking a sip from the orange coffee cup.

Mo' knew her mom was being an ass and depending on her response was the direction in which the conversation was going to go. Monday and Marcia bumped heads quite often and if you asked Dennis, it was because the pair was so much alike. To Monday, her mother was a stuck-up snob who acts as if she was too good for the world. Frowning down on anyone who didn't make eight figures. Marica was the true definition of a Hollywood bitch and Monday was the total opposite of that.

"Actually mother, I'm headed out to take care of some business before my flight in the morning. Is that okay with you?" Monday sassed, causing her mother to turn up her nose.

"Monday Charde Valentine, you better watch ya mouth before I watch it for you. I'm not one of yo lil' friends." Marcia hissed, warning her only daughter.

"Honey, calm down." Dennis turned to her and stated while the two most important women in his life participated in an intense stare down.

"Naw, don't tell me to calm down. I keep telling that damn girl that just cuz dem' lil white heffas she hangs with talk to their mothers like that.... I ain't been living in Cali all my life, she better recognize." Her mother continued to rant as she stood to her feet, preparing to leave for work.

Monday leaned against the kitchen counter listening to her mother snap on her and her dad. Marcia made it her business to remind them every chance that she got that she was different. Born and raised on the westside of Chicago in the North Lawndale area, Marcia, along with her twin sister Marsha, grew up with strict parents. The daughters of a pastor and first lady, they lived in church and with their heads in the books. Marcia was an Anesthesiologist and Marsha owned a high-end fashion boutique in downtown Chicago. When Monday's mom met Dennis on an online dating app, they hit if off fast and the next thing she knew, they were moving across the map. Landing a job at Pacific Shores Hospital and with Dennis already making big figures, Mo's life changed for the better.

"Ma, it's not that serious. I'll see you guys later." Monday finally spoke once her mom came up for air.

"Before you go, have you checked your flight itinerary and made sure that nothing has change? And what about luggage? I haven't seen you pack one bag and you leave tomorrow." Her dad chimed in as Monday made her way to the front door.

"No dad, everything is fine and I have packed the one bag I'm taking. I'll shop when I get there.... Love yall.... BYE!"

Monday rushed out of the house and to her black Mercedes Benz SL-Class, where she jumped in and dropped the top. Flipping her Gucci shades down over her eyes, she backed out of the driveway, ready to get her day started. Making her first stop at Capri Nail Spa, Monday was happy to see that Susan's pedicure chair was empty.

Getting the much-needed work done on her feet, she then switched seats, receiving a fill-in and color change. Monday and Susan caught up on each other's lives since their last encounter two weeks ago. Mo' revealed how excited she was to be graduating next year and heading to law school in the fall. She also gave her an ear full about her summer in Chicago and how she planned on living her best life. Transitioning from there, Monday made her way to Karen, her stylist, to get her lace front touched up before the flight in the morning. Just like with her nail tech, the two of them engaged in conversations surrounding everything from men to reality tv shows. Monday was really enjoying her day but started to feel sad when she realized it'll be months before she'd see any of them again. Making the best of her last visit, she stayed an hour after she was done running her mouth.

Finally, out the doors, Monday was in her car a few minutes before eight. Her entire day was gone but she got everything done, therefore, she didn't trip. Making her last stop at Chipotle, she jumped out and headed inside. Ordering two chicken bowls with everything and extra guacamole, she remembered to grab the drinks before exiting. Back inside her whip, she placed her phone on the dashboard while doing forty down residential streets. Arriving at the gated entrance, Monday turned down the music before pressing the intercom box. With no words being exchanged the gates opened, allowing her entrance. Cruising along the swirl driveway, she finally made it to her final destination. Killing the engine, Monday snatched up the food and hopped out, walking the short distance to the front door. Pulling on the door first, out of habit, she then rang the doorbell when she noticed that it was locked. Shifting her weight to one side, Monday let out a long sigh before ringing the bell again.

"Here I come." Martin called out from the other side just before pulling the door back.

Rolling her eyes to the back of her head, Monday tried pushing passed him, but he pulled her into a bear hug, making her completely forget about the fake attitude she had.

"Move, you knew I was on my way, yet you still took forever and a day to answer the door." She whined as he placed soft kisses on her neck.

"I'm sorry, beautiful. I was on a conference call with my dad and a few other bankers at the firm. You look beautiful. Let me get those for you." Martin apologized before grabbing the food out of her hands.

Leading her into the kitchen where he had a candlelight table for two waiting. Gushing on the inside and out, Monday blushed all the way over to her seat. Martin held out the chair for her before going inside the bags and placing the containers in front of them. Monday rested her elbow on the table and placed her chin inside the palm of her hands and smiled at her boyfriend of two years. Monday and Martin met at a party during summer break and she was immediately attracted to his pretty boys' ways. Standing tall at 6'3, Martin looked like the typical basketball player, however, he was the total opposite. An investment banker at his father's firm, Martin Gales was born into money and his ambitious ways in life guaranteed that he'd die with it.

"You know I could have had my chef come cook you up something special...."

"Special? You know how I feel about Chipotle and besides, it's already late. I don't need to be eating anything too heavy." Monday reached across the table, grabbed his hand, and stated.

Martin was the sweetest and Monday planned on marrying him one day, that one day being soon. Her parents loved and approved of him, he comes from a wealthy family, and if they could get help with one small issue, they'll be perfect.

"I can't believe you leaving me this summer." Martin told her before placing a fork full of rice in his mouth.

"Don't start baby and like I told you, you can fly out whenever to come visit. My cousin Shaq cool, so I know for a fact that she wouldn't trip about you staying there. We'll have a bathroom to ourselves and everything." Monday replied with a smile as bright as the sun.

She hoped like hell that he would consider flying out at least once while she was away. Martin and her best friend Kelly were the only people who'd she actually miss. Since telling her boyfriend about her plans to attend the internship in Chicago, he had been acting funny; in fact, he had been acting a lot like her mom.

"I just want you to be safe while you there Mo'. I see the news and they never have anything good to say about that place. The last thing I want is for you to get caught up in some type of shootout. You know it is always the innocent ones who get hurt...."

Martin rambled on and on until their food was disposed. Monday listened but chose not to respond; this had been a back and forth topic amongst them for the past month. He did everything in his power to convince her to stay, even offering to buy her everything under the moon but she declined. She was sick and tired of everyone in her life trying to control it. Only Monday knew what was best for Monday and it was time she proved that to the world.

"I'm just saying baby. I love you and ....."

Martin started back up but this time Mo' silenced him. Standing to her feet, she pulled off the crop top she wore, exposing her perfect C cups. Seductively gliding over towards him, Monday motioned for him to sit back before her long legs straddled him. This was their last night together for a few weeks and the last thing she wanted to do was argue. Placing a soft kiss on his lips, Monday made a trail with kisses to his ear before taking his earlobe into her mouth. She loved Martin more than he knew but she hated having to prove her love. Although he'd never admit it, Martin was extremely insecure; however, it was Monday's job as his woman to make sure that he wasn't.

"Listen baby. I love you and there's nothing a nigga from Japan to Chicago could do to take me away from you...." Monday promised but little did she know.

❧ 3 ❧

"**M**annnnn, BACK DOOR!" Law yelled before snapping his fingers and springing to his feet.

"You niggas run me my shit!" he boasted, snatching the hundred dollar bills out of Polo, Lil Keith, and Yayo's hands.

Participating in an intense dice game on the corner of Jackson and Kostner, Law ignored the stares from the police as they drove down the two-way street. They knew just like everyone else in the hood that the Jack Boyz ran everything from Jackson and Western down to Jackson and Austin and whatever side streets in between. It was rare for Law to stand out in public doing an activity as such, but it was the first ninety-degree day of the year and like everyone else in Chicago, he wanted to enjoy it.

"So, this what we doing now? Shooting dice and taking the lil niggas' money?" Law chuckled when he heard his best friend's voice in his ear.

"Nigga, I'll take yo son's money if he betting it up." He turned around and replied, coming face to face with Block.

"What up nigga!" the two said in unison before embracing in a manly hug.

Growing up next door to each other inside Rockwell Garden

Apartments, the two didn't have much choice but to be friends, seeing how their grandmothers were best friends as well. Law and Block, both were raised by strong black women who did whatever they could to provide for their families. When the factory closed and their grandmothers were laid off, the young thirteen-year-old friends took to the streets. Selling sawbuck and dime bags of weed at Westinghouse, the high school they attended, the two eventually got kicked out their junior year. With their heads already in the streets, Law and Block turned it up a few notches when they started fucking with that white girl. Earning respect from the big homies, the friends began to build their own empire in silence and knocked down whoever was in their way. With a group of loyal, hungry killers on their roster, there's no one man, group, gang, or organization that could stop the Jack Boyz.

"What you doing out? I thought Tisha had you on a six o'clock curfew?" Law noted as the two men walked over to the curb, where they rested on the hood of Law's midnight blue Porsche Cayenne.

"Tisha ain't got me on shit." Block smirked while pulling an already rolled backwood from behind his ear.

Law checked his phone for messages and missed calls while his homie sparked it up. Ignoring most of them, he was truly checking to see if Shaq had returned any of his calls or texts. Realizing that she hadn't, Law placed the iPhone back inside his pocket and focused on his surroundings. Hitting the blunt with two hard pulls, Block allowed the smoke to fill his lungs before releasing it into the air. Doing the same routine three more times, he passed the wood to Law before getting down to business.

"Them niggas out South acting like they wanna buss a move and---" Law began but was cut off by Block's deep voice.

"Then let 'em, we ain't ducking or dodging shit and in all honesty, if them niggas wanted smoke, shit..... look around nigga..... we ain't hard to find. We in these streets." Block told him before passing him that wood and lighting up another one.

It had been that way since they were kids. Law was the logical one while Block, on the other hand, was the irrational one. Their nicknames matching their personalities to a tee. Law, the handsome cut friend, reserved in appearance with his pretty boy looks and curly hair.

Block, on the other hand, was huge, with the height of a basketball player but with the weight of a football star, his body statue alone was intimidating. Both of them tatt'd like a subway in Harlem were on every bad bitch wish list.

"Aye, come take this ride with me to grab some food from Joe Willies and then we can do our rounds." Law tossed the roach and stated before getting inside his car while Block followed suit.

Heavy traffic flowed as Law impatiently waited to pull away from the curb. It seemed as if everybody in the Chi was outside, which only meant a bunch of homicides being reported on the news later. With the light turning red, Law was finally able to ease out after a white Audi 8. Doing a double take, he almost side swiped a car, trying to make sure his eyes wasn't deceiving him.

"Aint that's yo bitch?" Block noted, confirming Law's unsure thoughts.

"Yup!" he replied, bussing a sharp right behind her.

He hadn't spoken to Shaquita since she called herself putting him out and although it had only been a day, he knew that if he wanted to talk to her, he had to catch her in person.

"Nigga, you aight?" Law heard Block ask, causing him to chuckle as the truck leaned over on two wheels.

"Man, she ain't answering my calls and she think a muthafucker finna keep playing with her. Tell me why Hannah's old goofass gon' send her this old ass picture of me laying in her bed and nigga you know how Shaq is. I proposed to the girl and everything and ----"

"Again? Nigga, you proposed AGAIN?" Block blurted out and said in laughter while Law cut his eyes at him.

"Yeah.... AGAIN..... bitch! I love Shaquita and we were on a break when that photo was taken." Law defended himself as he jumped off the expressway at Independence.

"Well why the fuck you ain't just tell her that?"

"Cuz, I told her the last time I fucked her was the last time and it wasn't BUT STILL.... We were on a break."

Law filled Block in on everything going on between himself and Shaquita, all the while, still following her to her home. Staying at least two cars behind, he noticed someone in the passenger's seat but luckily for her, he could tell by the hair that it was another female.

"Aye, what you woulda did if that was a nigga in the car with shorty?" Block asked hypothetically as if he was reading Law's mind.

"It's only one call to the cleanup crew." Law looked over at him and snarled before shifting gears and double parking.

"Don't be getting no domestic nigga, it'll be a long weekend!" Block yelled out the window as Law stormed towards Shaquita.

Sneaking up on her as her and some chick pulled shopping bags after shopping bags out of the trunk of her car. Completely absorbed in conversation and girl talk, she didn't see him coming until it was too late.

"Oh my God, what the fuck you doing here Lawrence?" Shaquita rolled her eyes and asked before slamming her trunk shut.

"Cuz you childish and won't talk to me." He walked closer to her and replied, getting a better look at the young woman with her.

If Law hadn't known any better, he would have sworn that Shaquita had a twin sister that she never told him about. Both women stood about the same in height at 5'6; both built like your favorite Instagram model with wide hips and a slim waist. Shaquita was much thicker at the bottom than her friend, however, the beauty of them both were breathtaking.

"And I'll continue being childish. Enjoy your day Law. Let's go Monday." Shaq turned to face him and fumed before walking away, leaving him staring at her back.

Turning on his heels, Law headed back to the car more upset than he was when he got there. He knew for a fact that Shaquita would talk to him if she seen him in person but unfortunately for him, he was sadly mistaken. He couldn't help but wonder if she was truly fed up this time. The back and forth game between them weren't anything new and although Shaq thought he was out there bad, he had actually been a good boy.

"Guess that shit ain't go as planned." Block laughed the second Law got back inside the truck.

"Nigga fuck you." Law barked, shifting gears and pulling off into the flow of traffic.

He knew Block was ready with all the jokes, but he had other shit on his mind... like getting his bitch back. Letting down all the windows, Law turned up the sounds of Polo G and cruised the streets back to his side. He needed more smoke and some good advice if he planned on really making Shaq his wife.

❧ 4 ☙

"Aye, who was shorty with Shaquita yesterday?" Block hit the blunt and asked before releasing smoke circles in the air.

"What shorty?.... Ohhhhhh, that's her cousin Monday. I ain't never met her in person before but I know they like best friends and shit." Law answered from his spot on the couch inside of Block's basement.

"Nigga, why?" Block felt Law's eyes shift towards him and questioned, making him chuckle to himself.

"I'm just asking. I ain't never seen her around before and I thought I fucked all of Shaq's friends already." Block joked and the two laughed but they both knew there was truth behind his words.

"You talked to her yet?" Blocked looked away from the tv and questioned Law, who placed rubber bands on the bills that came out of the counting machine.

"Hell nah. I put some money in her account. She texted me saying, *thanks, but I don't need shit from yo bum ass,* and blocked me before I could write back." Law spoke in a serious tone, but Block couldn't help but laugh, him and Shaquita had a weird ass type of love.

"Shidddd, that's crazy Lord." Was all Block could say.

He wasn't in a position to give out advice when he was probably *thee* unhappiest nigga on Earth in a relationship. Sure, they both had women problems, but their relationship issues were very different. Together only about three years, Block considered what Law and Shaquita had as fresh. They were still in the honeymoon phase and at a point where they could work shit out. With him and Tisha, they had simply run their course and the both of them were unhappy' however, they stayed together because it's what *"families do."*

"BAEEEEEE!" Tisha's voice rang out through the basement, causing both men eyes to shift towards the stairs.

Without replying, Tisha called out to him one last time before she appeared in the doorway of his man cave. Block glanced up at her, giving her a full look over before focusing back on *The Call of Duty* game in front of him.

"So, you ain't hear me call yo big head ass?" Tisha snapped, stomping towards him, standing in front of the flat screen tv mounted on the wall.

"Move the fuck out the way." He told her, never taking his eyes off the game.

"But what up?" He asked, his eyes raised high towards the sky as he battled for a victory.

"Can you drop AJ off at my momma house for me?" Tisha smacked her lips and asked, causing Block's face to frown.

"Over yo momma house for what?" he glanced over at her before passing the game controller to Law.

"Aye, play this for me." He requested, standing to his feet, towering over the mother of his child.

"Why he going over yo momma house? Didn't she just have him last weekend?" Block asked her with a raised eyebrow.

"Yeah that's cuz I was in Miami with my girls last weekend and this weekend we are celebrating Vonna's birthday so...."

"So, you need to tell them to count you out this weekend. You need to spend some time with your son instead of partying and shit." Block explained to her as if she didn't already know.

"TIME? THE NERVE OF YOU NIGGA! You barely home spending time with us so you need to shut the fuck up and ..."

"And you need to watch yo muthafuckn' mouth." He stepped closer to her and roared, causing even Law to look in his direction.

"The issue is that I'm not home with YOU, but I tuck my son in EVERY night. I hustle in the streets and at the shop so you can sit on yo ass and shop all day. You had *one* job, be a good mother to my son and you can have whatever in the world whether we together or not but instead, you wanna party and shake yo ass for snapchat every day." Block went on to say while Tisha's eyes began to water.

"Aye bruh, Imma head up outta here. I'll meet up with you later." Law stood to his feet and announced, placing the controller in his hands on the cream ottoman in front of him.

"Aight bro." Block agreed with a head nod before focusing his attention back on the woman he once was madly in love with.

Block and Tisha met in the eighth grade when she moved into the projects. Loving everything about her the moment they were introduced, Block quickly made Tisha his girl, eventually taking her virginity and giving her a son. Like with every couple and in every relationship, they had their share of problems but regardless of how big it was, they overcame it. Everything changed about a year after Tisha gave birth to his Junior, Aaron Williams II. It seemed as if the whole dynamic of their relationship shifted and of course, they each blamed the other. Making a promise to fight for their family no matter what, their son was turning five in September, making it five years of pure hell.

"Look, have fun. I'll keep AJ with me." Block finally broke the silence and stated before walking around her and up the stairs.

Going to the second landing of the house they shared, Block entered his son's bedroom where he found him lounging in his game chair playing Roblox. Stepping back, he admired his creation from afar and smiled. Out of all Block's wrongs, his son made up for it and he planned on being the best father to him as he could.

"What up boy, what ya doing?" Block walked in and announced himself, giving him a love tap on the back of the dome.

"Ouch Dad. You just made me get out." AJ turned around and frowned, rubbing the back of his head.

"That's cuz ya ass weak!" Block laughed before taking a seat on the full-size bed inside of his gamer themed bedroom.

"Put ya shoes on, come take this ride with me." He finished up saying while AJ sprung to his feet searching his closet for a pair of shoes.

"Look Dad, Imma rock my Mikes like you!" He exclaimed, holding the classic pair of red and black flu games in the air.

Chuckling to himself, Block shook his head up and down and watched his boy move about the room trying his hardest to mimic his outfit. Both dressed in a pair of black distressed jeans, AJ threw on a white wife beater, just like his. Block continued to watch as his son headed over to the dresser where he grabbed his brush.

"I'm ready, Daddy." AJ announced, brushing the motion sick waves that rested on his head.

"Where yo chain?"

"Ah, I almost forgot. Hold on." He replied, holding up one finger in the air as he made his way over to the dresser.

"Aight. How I look?" AJ flexed, causing Block to bend over in laughter.

"Like a lil boss, grab yo fitted and let's ride."

Blocked watched as his son move about the room searching for his red and black Chicago Bulls fitted cap. Finding it on top of his toy chest, he then ran across to the other side of the room where he grabbed his phone off the charger as well.

"Nigga, who gon' call you?" Block stood in the doorway and quizzed AJ, who only smiled before taking off down the stairs.

Staying close behind him, Block made his way down as well, stopping first off in the kitchen to grab him a bottle of water and AJ a blue Gatorade. He planned on getting them something to eat a little later but for now, they needed to stay hydrated.

"Aye bruh, I'm about to leave yo as—"

Block paused when AJ came running at top speed into the kitchen, almost colliding with his knees. It wasn't his son's appearance that froze his words, it was Tisha's, who came walking up behind him.

"So......where we going? Should I change my shoes?" She asked in a quirky tone that threw him for a loop.

"Me and my Junior 'bout to slide out. Let's go!" Block tapped AJ upside the back his head, ushering him towards the door.

"Ok, so I *should* change then? Wait. Let me put on my Mikes too." She beamed, turning on her heels heading up the stairs.

"But I thought you already had plans? Ain't it's Vonna's birthday or sum shit?" Block hinted, referring to the conversation they recently had.

"Yeah but that was before I knew ---"

"Nah we good love, enjoy." Block stressed, cutting her off in mid-sentence before leaving her standing in the kitchen alone.

❧ 5 ❧

"Girl, fuck that job and call off...."

"Call off? Girl, yo vacation starts Friday, take yo ass in and make that money."

"OKAY! OKAY! OKAY!" Shaquita yelled aloud before kicking the lavender sheets from off top of her and jumping out of the bed.

She laid in there for almost twenty-minutes listening to her good conscious and bad conscious go back and forth. She hated Monday mornings, she wasn't the biggest fan of her job either, but money made her cum and Planned Parenthood kept her bussing.

Heading straight to the bathroom, Shaq started the shower before washing her face and brushing her teeth at the sink. Once she was done there, she joined the steam and hot water inside the standup shower. Washing her body twice with her favorite Peppermint Dr. Bronner's soap, she then rinsed off and got out. Grabbing the pink and yellow dry towel off the rack, Shaquita wrapped it around her and exited the bathroom. The sound of the central air cranking let her know that it was hot out, making her want to call off even more.

Going inside the drawers, Shaq pulled out a matching pantie and bra set as well as a blue and yellow SpongeBob smock. Applying lotion from head to toe, Shaquita then threw on her clothes, placed her long honey blonde thick hair up in a high bun before sliding in her crocs. Stopping at the full-length mirror inside her closet, Shaq did a full spin, looking herself over one last time before leaving out. Stopping at the second door from the laundry room, Shaquita knocked softly twice before Monday's voice rang from the other side. Slowly cracking it open, Shaquita smiled at the sight of her favorite cousin. Although she's been in town for a few days, things still seemed surreal.

"DID I WAKE YOU?" SHAQUITA WALKED IN AND ASKED WHILE Monday sat up straight in the King size bed.

"NOPE! MARTIN CALLED ME BEFORE BOARDING HIS FLIGHT TO Germany this morning, and I haven't been able to fall back to sleep since then." Monday replied before continuing.

"YOU LOOK ALL CUTE OR WHATNOT. WHAT TIME YOU GET OFF?"

WALKING COMPLETELY INSIDE THE ROOM, SHAQUITA TOOK A SEAT on the edge of the bed before letting out a loud dramatic sigh.

"WHAT?" MONDAY GIGGLED WHILE SHAQ FLOPPED BACK ON THE mattress.

"I DON'T WANNA GOOOOOO...... IT'S THE SUMMERTIME.... THE niggas with money out and Imma be helping bitches who should've kept they muthafuckn' legs closed!" Shaquita screamed out, sending Monday into a laughing frenzy.

"GIRL, IT'S OKAY. THIS YOUR LAST WEEK. I'M THE ONE WHO SHOULD be crying. I start this internship tomorrow and I really don't wanna go."

"YOU SHUT UP! IT'S ONLY THREE DAYS OUT THE WEEK FOR LIKE FOUR hours, you'll be okay while me on the other hand..." Shaq paused, sitting up and standing to her feet.

"I GOTTA DEAL WITH THESE HATING ASS OLDER BITCHES AT MY JOB and these lil hoes with attitudes all day." Shaquita finished before letting out another loud sigh.

"PRAY FOR ME COUSIN." SHE GROANED BEFORE TURNING ON HER heels and walking completely out the house.

ONCE INSIDE THE CAR, SHAQ TOSSED HER NIKE BOOKBAG ON THE passenger's seat, connected the Bluetooth, rolled down all windows, and headed towards the Loop. With school being out for the summer, her drive down 290 was a breeze. Summer Walker's latest LP blasted through her ride, giving off the exact vibe she needed to get through the workday. Parking inside the employees' lot, Shaquita looked across the street at the visitor's lot and shook her head. It was barely nine and the place was packed already, sending her energy back down.

"IT'S OKAY FRIEND. WE GON' GET THROUGH THESE EIGHT HOURS together. Come on." Daisy appeared out of nowhere and stated, locking arms with a stunned Shaq.

"WHAT YOU DOING HERE? I THOUGHT YOU WAS OFF TODAY." Shaquita replied, brightening up a bit as the two walked arm and arm inside of work.

"I WAS BUT I SWITCHED WITH PEDRO." DAISY EXPLAINED WHILE they clocked in at the computer near the back desk.

"I AIN'T TRIPPING THOUGH CUZ DON NEM'S PARTY FRIDAY NIGHT and I can sleep in late Saturday." She continued while Shaquita looked over the schedule and appointments for the day.

"AND SPEAKING OF DON'S PARTY.... YOU COMING RIGHT?"

SHAQUITA'S EYES SHIFTED SLOWLY FROM THE COMPUTER IN FRONT OF her over to her friend/co-worker. She remembered telling Daisy that she'd go with her but that was before her and Law got into it. Don was also a Jack Boy and she knew for a fact that her ex-boyfriend would be in attendance. Shaquita hadn't spoken to, seen, or heard from Law since the day Monday arrived from California. She knew that he was still somewhere lurking in the cut but she preferred to keep her distance and going to his homie's party was not doing that.

"OKAY SO WHAT HAD HAPPENED WAS…."

"SHAQUITA VALENTINE! NO! I AIN'T TRYING TO HEAR THAT!" Daisy followed Shaq inside one of the recovery rooms and growled.

"YOU PROMISED ME THAT AND ---"

"AND I AIN'T TRYING TO BE AROUND THAT NIGGA. YOU AS MY friend should understand that." Shaq cut her off and stated.

"I DO BUT DO YOU THINK HE AVOIDING PARTIES AND SHIT BECAUSE of you? You think he's stopping his fun? Anddddddd poor Monday, she stuck in the house with yo ass. Child ain't never been to Chicago and this how she spending her time…. Running away from everything involving Law?"

DAISY RAMBLED ON AND ON, LAYING IT HEAVY ON THE GUILT TRIP and luckily for her, it was working. In reality, she was avoiding Law but that was impossible when him and his team were everywhere. On top of promising Daisy that she'd go, she promised Monday a good time in her city and here she was reneging on it all.

"OKAY. OKAY. I'LL GO FRIDAY BUT BITCH, IF I CATCH A DOMESTIC at this pool party, Imma ….."

THE SOUND OF THE BACK-DESK PHONE RINGING FROZE HER WORDS AS she looked down at the caller ID.

"HOLD ON, IT'S THE FRONT DESK." SHAQ TOLD HER, HOLDING UP HER finger in the air before answering it.

"ME? OKAY, HERE I COME." SHE SMILED, SLAMMING DOWN THE receiver and moving from around the desk.

"WHAT THEY WANT? WHAT SHE SAY?" DAISY QUIZZED AS SHE followed behind Shaquita with hopes on solving the mystery.

THE TWO WOMEN WALKED THROUGH THE CLINIC HEADING TO THE front desk. Shaquita ignored the questions coming from Daisy as she spoke to other coworkers in passing. She loved Daisy's feisty Latin personality, but the girl knew how to work her nerves. Friends since nursing school, they had grown really close over the years and Shaq wouldn't trade in her girl for nothing in the world.

"OH MY GOD! ARE THOSE YOURS?" DAISY BEAMED AS SHE STOOD ON the side of Shaquita, staring at a large box of customized Venus et Fleur roses.

"YUUUUPPPPP....." SHE SNICKERED, PICKING UP THE CARD THAT rested on the five-hundred dollar roses.

I'M TRYING TO GET IT RIGHT MAN. I LOVE YOU SHAQUITA AND I miss you but most importantly, a nigga SORRY!
   -Law

SHAKING HER HEAD BACK AND FORTH, SHAQ PLACED THE CARD IN her smock pocket, picked up the black box, and took it to her station in the back. Roses was a first for Law; he wasn't the romantic type and his idea of apologizing was buying her a bag. She gave him an A for effort, but she wasn't impressed; she needed changed behavior, nothing more, nothing less. The rest of the workday flew by, especially with the heavy flow of patients. Barely taking a lunch break Shaquita couldn't have been happier when five-thirty finally came around. Leaving the lavender roses on her desk, Shaquita grabbed everything else, including her phone and heading out the door. Clocking out with Daisy the same way they clocked in, the two headed out the doors, going their separate ways. Walking through the first parking lot, Shaquita stopped just as the light turned red, leaving her and a few other pedestrians waiting patiently. Glancing down at her phone, the light finally changed green, allowing them to across. With her head now held high, she strutted down the crosswalk in front of a candy apple red BMX 5 Series truck.

"Excuse me miss." She heard a voice say but she refused to look back; it was rush hour traffic and all she wanted to do was get home.

"Excuse me miss." The same voice rang out again just as she stepped foot on the curb.

The same as last time, Shaquita ignored him and everybody else around her. She had tunnel vision and the only thing in her sight was her car, which would eventually lead her to her bed. Seeing the pot of gold at the end of the rainbow, Shaq hit the alarm on her Audi and smiled to herself, she was almost there. Pushing it forward, Shaq thought she was out of the clear when she heard the same man's voice again, this time it was much closer. Spinning around on her heels, Shaquita prepared to face the stranger and let him down gently.

"Hi sir but I'm not intere----"

Shaq's words froze the moment she laid eyes on the fellow jogging in her direction. Dressed in a pair of light jeans, loose laced Timbs, and a purple and gold Kobe jersey, Shaquita couldn't help but lust over his swollen tatt'd arms that rested shirtless under the fabric. His dreads were pulled to the back in a rubber band and the gold Rolex on his wrist glistened under the sun. Completely stunned by his looks, Shaquita remained quiet and waited for him to fully approach her.

"Damn, you gon' kill a nigga before he even get yo number." He winced, pulling out a blue inhaler and taking two hard pulls from it.

It was the cutest thing Shaq had ever seen. Here he was, fine as Michael B Jordan with the swag of The Game, yet he was taking pulls from an asthma pump like Steve Urkel. Laughing to herself, Shaquita waited and watched him pull it together.

"You okay?" she giggled, looking him up and down as he put the inhaler away.

"I'm straight, I know if I fall out, I'm in the presence of a nurse." He noted with a grin, sending her pussy on a throbbing mission.

"What's ya first name Nurse Valentine?" He continued, reaching forward, flickering her ID badge.

"I'm Shaquita and you are...."

Shaq's words were cut short when she heard a female's voice yelling from across the street. Her eyes darting in the direction, she noticed a woman standing in front of the truck he was in, screaming.

"Weezy! Weezy!" she yelled as the noise from car horns sounded loudly through the streets.

"Is she calling you?" Shaq turned to the mystery man and asked.

"Yeah, that's my lil sister. I stopped traffic to talk to you.... All dem muthafuckers can wait though." Weezy told her, waving off the angry people who cursed and fussed.

Taking his number with promises to call him later, Shaquita switched away to her car. It wasn't like her to entertain random men, but If Law didn't act right, she knew a new nigga who would.

Monday danced in the bathroom mirror to City Girl's latest hit, *Act Up*, while she applied a coat of Fenty Lip Gloss to her full set of lips. It was Friday night and after the first week of internship, she looked forward to this party. When Shaq came home earlier in the week and told her about it, Monday was beyond ecstatic to further learn that it was a pool party. Dressed in a two-piece Burberry swimsuit, Monday unbuttoned the white jean shorts she wore on top and secured her diamond belly ring in place before walking out. Pulling the matching Burberry flip flops out of the box, she then grabbed her silk scarf and placed it on top of her soft big curls. Walking back inside the bathroom, Monday tied the Burberry scarf perfectly and fixed the long flowy weave underneath.

"You a bad bitch Mo'!" she smiled at her reflection in the mirror and beamed just as the sound of her phone ringing replaced the music in the background.

Giving herself one final stare, she blew out an air kiss before heading back inside the bedroom to retrieve her phone. Stepping over the clothes and shoes that blocked her path, she finally made it to the bed, just before the voicemail picked up.

"Hey mom." She spoked, flopping down on the bed and grabbing the bottle of baby oil that rested on the nightstand.

"Monday! What are you doing?" her mother yelled just as the music started up again.

Jumping to her feet, she ran across the room and shut the door before replying back to her mom.

"I just got out the shower. We're playing music and making pizza. We're having a movie night." She lied with a smile planted across her caramel complexed face.

"How's your stay been thus far? You had a famous Chicago Dog yet?" She heard her father say, letting her know the call was on speaker.

"Nope. Not yet Dad. Maybe when we go to the Taste of Chicago or something but not yet." She replied to him, taking the dry towel, removing the excess oil off her body.

"Well we talked to Martin. He called to check up on us, even in Germany." Her mother started and Monday knew exactly where she was headed.

"Why is it that he can call to check on us and our own daughter, who's not even in another country, can't? You answer your phone here and there and..."

"Ma, when you call, I be working. I can't just answer my phone." Monday cut her off and stated, rolling her eyes to the back of her head.

This was the exact reason she didn't answer their calls or text messages. They were overprotective and overbearing, which was too much for her. Monday knew how lucky and blessed she was; however, she didn't need her parents reminding her every nine minutes. It was the summertime and all she wanted to do was have fun, nothing more and nothing less. She was killing it her first week at work and although her and Shaq did nothing but shop and sleep, it was now time to live a little.

"Martin told us how he planned on visiting you when he got back. I think that'll be great for the both of you to experience the culture together." Daniel chimed in once Marcia came up for air.

"Culture? Dad, it's Chicago, Illinois, not Hong Kong, the culture ain't that damn different...."

"Ohhh, so you cursing now in Chicago?" Marcia's voice overpowered Daniel's, causing Monday to laugh aloud.

"Ma? Really Ma?" she questioned as she listened to them tussle over control of the phone in their background.

"Seriously, Monday, listen to me. Although the culture may not differ much in your eyes, it is not the same. You have to be built a certain way to live in those Chicago streets or they'll eat you up alive. You listen to the music, the people there, they live it and it's not like you see on tv. I need you to be careful and by careful, I mean, no standing in large crowds, never ever just sit in a parked car, stay off 16th street, and absolutely no public transportation. If Shaq is unable to drive you herself then call an Uber... As a matter of fact, rent a car Monday because....."

"Oh my God, bye ma!" Mo yelled, ending the call just as Shaquita burst through the door laughing.

"Girl, you grown as fuck, still lying to them people."

"Was you listening at the door?" Monday jumped to her feet and asked, placing both hands on her hips as her cousin bent over in laughter.

"Bitch talm 'bout ..... yes master, we having a movie night." Shaquita replied in her best slave impersonation.

"Girl fuck you! You ready to go?" Monday snorted before tossing a decorative pillow at her head.

"Am I ready? Chile do you see me?" Shaq boasted, doing a full spin showing off her one piece Chanel bathing suit with the matching slide in sandals.

Monday quickly turned around and grabbed her phone off the bed. Going directly to her favorite app, Snapchat, she began flicking pictures and videos of her cousin. With no need for a filter, Monday boosted her head up, playing the part of her cheerleader. Shaquita was in fact a bad bitch and Monday loved when they hit the town together, they turned heads near and far.

"I was gon' wear my two piece but the way this ass is set up!" Shaq noted, doing a light twerk in the mirror on the side of the door.

The two women participated in a quick twerk session before gathering the last of their things and walking out the door. Once inside the car, Shaquita placed the address in the GPS as Monday buckled herself in. Pulling down the sun visor, she checked her reflection and made sure her jewelry was in place before closing it shut. Rolling down the windows so that the hot leather seats wouldn't melt her skin, Monday was ready to get her night started.

"Damn, why the fuck Don gotta have this party all the way out in the 200s? I hate out south man." Shaquita winced before placing a call to Daisy, who was meeting them there.

Sitting back in her seat, Monday halfway listened to their conversation as thoughts about life back at home invaded her mind. It had only been a week and she was already starting to feel a little home sick. She was enjoying Shaq's company; however, she was out of her comfort zone. Trying her best to shake those thoughts, Monday was thankful that Shaquita ended her call and turned up the music because the ratchet sounds of Kash Doll plugged her ears and her mind. Rapping along to each word, the two enjoyed the playlist the entire hour ride, making the transition a much smoother one.

"Damn, we really gon' have to park all the way down here." Shaq fussed as she circled the block for a third time.

Monday sat in a daze, impressed at how many expensive cars lined the streets. When Shaquita briefed her on who the Jack Boyz were, she mentioned that they were paid but Monday had no clue she meant like this. Settling on a space a block away, they both exited the car to begin their hike to the mansion. Locking hands, Shaquita and Monday laughed at the men who held up traffic, trying to get their attention. Monday could tell by the flow of people heading towards the house that it was going to be a night to remember.

"There go Daisy right there." Shaq noted, pointing across the street at a thick Puerto Rician chick with blonde hair.

The two stood still and waited as Daisy dodged traffic and thirsty gawks from the men driving by. Both Shaquita and Monday laughed while she stuck up her middle finger and cursed in Spanish the entire way over to them.

"Fuckn' Cono!" she hissed, stepping unto the curb and giving Shaq a huge hug.

"Oh my God, you must be Monday. You are gorgeous. Nice to

finally meet you." Daisy turned to Mo and babbled, pulling her into an embrace as well.

"Nice to meet you too." Mo smiled before the now trio made their way to the first official party of the summer.

Using the front door as their choice of entrance, the girls held hands as they navigated through the crowded yet spacious mansion. Monday's eyes roamed freely, checking out everything, near and far. A few people hung out in the kitchen while a gang of others sat around the pool table. It seemed as if all eyes were planted on them, however, there were bad bitches swarming around. Never a hater, Monday admired a couple, even giving off a few friendly stares but there was no doubt in her mind that she was the baddest bitch in there.

"There go Don over there. Let's go wish him a happy birthday." Shaq instructed, pointing across the lawn as they stood at the patio door.

Walking in a single file line, from shortest to tallest, Daisy greeted the bald-headed gentleman first with a hug. Monday's eyes bucked as his big hands gripped her round ass; however, from the giggles from Daisy, she seemed to be enjoying it.

"What up Shaq?" He said in a deep voice, only giving her half the hug he had just given her friend.

"Damn.... And who the fuck is this with yall?" Don questioned, staring Monday up and down like he was undressing the little clothes she did have on with his eyes.

"This my cousin Monday but she's off limits. Happy birthday nigga!" Shaq retorted, pulling Monday away by the arm as everyone nearby laughed.

Heading towards the DJ booth that sat tucked off in a corner near the back, Monday's hips swayed to the music as she watched butt naked women jump in the hot tub. Shaking her head from side to side, she was embarrassed for them as they allowed men to smack them on the ass. It seemed as if nowadays women didn't know how to be bad bitches without being hoes too. Reaching the bar on the opposite side, Shaq turned to her girls before flagging down the bartender.

"What y'all drinking?"

"I'll take a Long Island; I'm trying to keep it cute tonight." Daisy smacked her lips and replied while pulling her hair behind her ears.

"I'll take the same." Monday spoke up and answered next before Shaquita turned back around and placed their order.

It seemed as if the bartender had their drinks on standby, how fast they got them. Taking her first sip, the strong liquor hit her like a drink with no chaser. Monday watched and laughed as both Shaquita and Daisy had the exact same reaction. Taking a few more sips, the girls grooved to the music and scoped out the place.

"Look at Don over there, acting a fool." Shaq said, pointing across the backyard at the birthday boy who was practically getting head in front of the entire party.

Monday had been to plenty of kickbacks but none of them like this. White kids high off drugs partied a little bit differently. And then you had those rich people parties where they got high off some whole other shit. Nonetheless, she was enjoying herself and happy to be there.

"So, Mo', girl.... How long you here for?" Daisy asked through sips from the little black straw.

"The beginning of September." Monday replied as her eyes followed Shaquita's eyes, wondering who she was staring at.

"That nigga bet not come back over here trying to mack and shit." Shaq growled, referring to Don.

"Girl stop hating and let Monday have some fun. You know them niggas gon' make sure she straight." Daisy chimed in while Shaquita's eyes cut into her.

"She already straight. She's here for school and to have fun, but I refuse to let her fuck around and get involved with a Jack Boy and....." Shaquita snapped, only for her words to get lost and replaced by the presence of two fine ass men.

7

"What about dem' Jack Boyz?" Block walked up with Law and asked, his eyes automatically focusing in on Shaquita's cousin, Monday.

"I saidddddddd, that Y'ALL ain't shit and ...."

"And we ain't finna do this right here. Let me holler at you." Law interrupted her in a calm tone before pulling her away.

Watching his homie and his girl fight always seemed to make Block laugh. He never understood why they put on a show, only to be right back fucking around with each other. Always the one to mind his business, Block kept his mouth shut and all his thoughts to himself. Speaking of minding his business, he turned his attention back to both ladies who stood near him as well as Don, who was now in their presence. Even prettier close up, Block hadn't noticed the freckles on her nose from the car or the deep dimple that was only in one cheek. A little pudge in her stomach let him know her body was real and with all the fake asses skating around, niggas was thankful for that nowadays. She was a real beauty and in all of Block's twenty-five years on Earth, he had never been mesmerized, until now.

"Aye, they got a smoke room in there. Come with me." Block

tapped Monday on the elbow and said, however, he was speaking generally.

Pulling a rolled backwood from behind his ear, he led the group through the house and to a room Law told him about earlier. Checking for his pistol out of habit, Block knew he was surrounded by love, but snakes had a way of blending in.

"Aye, close the door." He said to Don before taking a seat on the brown leather sectional in the dim room.

Lighting the wood, Block hit the exotic weed three times before passing it to Daisy, who was practically sitting on his lap. With all the space available in the room, she chose to be under him, but he wasn't complaining. He knew Daisy from around the way; she was pretty much the only thick Puerto Rican bitch in the hood, therefore, she stood out like a sore thumb. Other than seeing her with Shaquita a few times, he really didn't know much about her.

"Nah, I'm good!" Monday's soft voice spoke, awakening Block from his thoughts.

Glancing over at her, he watched as she rejected the blunt before passing it to Don. To him, she was the prettiest woman walking the Earth and he had been to over 10 countries. It was something about her that screamed, *different*. She spoke differently, her accent, the way she pronounced each syllable in every word. Her tone was soft when he was used to a more aggressive sound. She was well-mannered and more attractive than what the eye beholds.

"Aw, so you don't smoke? I forgot you was Miss UCLA or whatever!" Daisy shaded before rolling her eyes and looking away.

"No baby, it's *STANFORD UNIVERSITY,* but nice try." Monday snapped back, giving Daisy a full stare down.

Chuckling aloud, Block found himself being turned on by her feistiness and he could tell by Daisy's demeanor that she wasn't expecting that response either. He hated being around or involved in female cattiness, but Daisy was looking for trouble.

"Stanford University huh? Ain't they like one of the top schools in the nation?" Block asked, reaching forward and grabbing the blunt from Don.

" We number 2, BABY!" Monday sassed, cutting her eyes in Daisy's direction again.

"That's what's up? Congratulations sweetheart!" he turned to her and smiled before releasing smoke through his nostrils.

"What you in school for? When you graduate?" Block continued and asked.

"I graduated last month but I'll attend Stanford Law in the fall." Monday replied with a smile, locking eyes with him for the first time that night.

"Word? Lawyer, huh? That's dope!" Don added in while Block continued to stare from across the room.

"So, how long you in Chicago?" Don followed up and quizzed, asking all the questions Block wanted to know the answers to.

"Just until September. I'm interning at a law firm downtown for a month and then I'm going to just finish the summer out here."

"Word! You got a nigga back in Cali?" Don boldly asked, causing Block to shake his head back and forth.

"Well.... Ummmm.... Yes, I do have a man back home." Monday hesitantly answered, pulling her eyes away from Block's.

"Fuck dat nigga. Bet he a lame. Let me be yo Chicago Summertime Thug." Don stood to his feet and said with conviction, sending everyone in the small room in an uproar.

"Nigga, sit yo goofass down. Monday's good.... Ain't you Monday?" Block turned to her and asked, looking her deep in the eyes.

"Yeah, I'm goo—"

The sound of loud voices and the door being pushed open silenced Monday. Everyone's eyes in the room bucked as they watched Tisha and her cousin Vonna crash their smoking session. Not only wasn't she supposed to be in there, she wasn't invited to the party at all. Shaking his head from side to side, Block knew what type of night he was in for and regretted even leaving the house in the first place.

"Why the fuck is this bitch on yo lap?" Tisha snapped, charging towards them, but Block jumped to his feet to block her passage.

"Do it look like she on my fuckn' lap? What you doing here? And then acting all stupid and shit?" Block looked her in the eyes and asked.

"NO! The question is, why every time it's some bitches around, they all in yo face? And Don...." Tisha turned to him and said with her hands placed on her hips.

"Why the fuck you ain't invite me to yo party?"

Tisha was known to pop up and cause a scene, which was something that Block thought was cute, five years ago. With them now being five years from thirty, it was time she chilled out on the hood rat shit. She was still the feisty, smart mouthed, down for whatever, ride or die girl he fell in love with, but that was the problem. She hadn't grown much over the years and Block partially blamed himself for that. He should have moved on years ago, but he couldn't walk away from his son. Growing up with only a grandmother, he always vowed to have the family that he wasn't born into. He promised not only himself but Tisha and his son as well that he'll be around for them, no matter what.

"This is EXACTLY why he ain't invite yo silly ass. You too old for this shit man..... Let's GO!" Block barked, spinning Tisha around by her shoulders as she stomped out the door.

It had been a while since he felt a sense of embarrassment, however, at that very moment, he was ashamed. He knew for a fact that any chances he had with Monday went out the window, just by the look on her face. Continuing to keep it cool, Block ushered his baby mother out the door but not before turning to Monday.

"It was nice meeting you, baby." He said with a wink of an eye before escorting Tisha out the party, silently wishing it was his life instead.

❦ 8 ❦

The vibration from his phone tucked under the pillow woke Law along with the rays of sun that peeked from behind the thin curtains. Feeling for the device with his hands, he finally retrieved it and checked his messages. With a few missed calls and notifications from ESPN, he didn't find anything important, therefore, he placed it on the charger and rolled over. A smile crept across his face as he laid eyes on the most beautiful woman in the world. With a little slob dripping from her mouth and a few light snores, Shaquita was still everything to him. The night before when he ran into her at the party, Law took her to the car, where they had a heart to heart. He had been sick without his girl the past week, which only confirmed how much he thought he loved her. Showing Shaquita receipts in the form of text messages between him and the girl he supposedly cheated with, Law proved to her that the girl was clout chasing and it wasn't what it seemed. Thankful that she forgave him, they left the party early, and came back to her place where he fucked her brains out.

"I'm ready for round two." He mumbled to himself before pulling the sheets back off of Shaquita and prying her legs apart.

"Stopppp. What you doing?" she squirmed in her sleep, fake fighting him off.

"Shhhhh.....It's breakfast time." He looked up from between her legs and said before diving deep in between them.

Law's tongue worked its magic, making her come within less than a minute. With her legs shaking uncontrollably, Shaq practically fought him away as he went back in for seconds. He laughed at her antics before jumping out of the bed and heading to the shower. As bad as Law wanted to go for a round two, he had to meet Block at the shop by one. Turning on the shower and then heading back to the sink, he smiled when he noticed his toothbrush still in the same spot. He knew that him and Shaquita wasn't done and it felt good knowing that she knew the same. Brushing his teeth, Law finished up at the sink before getting inside the shower. Positioning himself directly under the showerhead, Law closed his eyes and allowed the hot water to take control. The sound of the toilet flushing caused those same eyes to pop open before he pulled back the shower curtain. Law watched Shaquita's head to the sink where she brushed her teeth as well. Taking a swig from the mouthwash in the cabinet, Law continued to watch her as she pulled the t-shirt she wore over her head.

"MOVE!" She ordered, pulling back the curtains and getting inside the steamy shower with him.

With his dick harder than before, Law wasted no time and said no words; instead, he bent Shaquita over and guided his nine and half inches inside of her. Her hands slipped as she tried to grab the wall to maintain her balance. Shaq's loud moans sent him over the edge, causing him to pick up his speed.

"Fuckkkk... I'm finna cum!" Shaquita moaned out as the two came together, ending their shower quickie.

"Whew! That was good. Now wash up and get out so I can turn the hot water up." Shaquita turned around to him and requested before pushing him forward so he could do as she told.

Law washed up twice before getting out and drying off with the fluffy yellow towel that waited for him on the rack. Grabbing a pair of Nike shorts he left behind, Law spotted Shaq's Bath and Body Works lotion on the dresser and headed over to it. Flipping the top back, he smelled the Champagne Toast scented moisturizer and began applying it on his chest and arms. Satisfied with the fragrance, he then slipped on a pair of all white air force ones, grabbed his keys and phone off the charger before hollering out to his girl.

"I'm gone bae. I'll be back over later." Law yelled over the running water as he made his way out the bedroom door and down the stairs.

"What's up shorty!" He spoke, greeting Monday who was heading up with a bowl of fruit in her hands.

"Hello. Good Morning." She replied with a smile before sashaying passed him.

Out of habit, Law turned around and watched her ass bounce up and down before she disappeared in one of Shaquita's guest rooms. Shaking his head from side to side, scenes from the movie *Player's Club* played in his mind as he stepped into the blazing sun. With no shirt or socks on, Law still felt like he was in the middle of a desert. Trickles of sweat threatened to fall from his forehead as he made his way to his car. Wasting no time, Law rolled down all the windows before cutting the air conditioner on high. Plugging his phone up to the aux cord, Pop Smokes hit song *"Dior"* came blasting through the speakers first. Turning the volume up a few notches, Law slowly backed out of Shaquita's driveway, heading to his first destination of the day. Jumping on 290, Law drove to the hood but not before stopping at BP gas station for a pack of blunts. Grabbing that along with a bottle of water, he drove another two minutes before pulling in front of The Jack Shop.

"What's up muthafuckers!" Law walked in and yelled loudly, making sure everyone in the establishment heard him.

"What up fool?" Tory, his barber, spoke up first followed by different greetings from the other men in the barber shop.

"Nigga don't be walking in my shit with all dat noise." Block appeared from his back office and barked while Law took a seat in Tory's chair.

Per usual, business for Block was booming. Men waited for hours to get lined up by the best barbers on the westside of Chicago. Of course, Law didn't have an issue with waiting, especially seeing how his right hand man was the owner.

"Aye, what happen to you last night? I seen you pulling Tisha out by her collar and shit." Law joked, referring to the last time he seen him at the pool party.

"Mannnn.... That's some shit I don't even wanna talk about. That muthatfuckn' girl there!" Block shook his head from side to side and winced.

Law and Block had been friends long enough for Law to know that his homie was tired and at his ends with his baby mother. They had been trying since they've been kids but unfortunately, they couldn't get it right. Tisha was a hood rat, doing hood rat shit with her friends and at twenty-five, she was too old for that. Law never understood why Block didn't move around. Every bitch that knew him wanted him but for some reason, he played them all to the left.

"What happened with you and Shaquita?" Block asked, changing the subject while Tory placed the cape around his neck.

"I just left from over there. We good. As a matter of fact, I'm about to stop playing before I lose her. She been asking me to get my number changed and I've been thinking about doing it. I know the type of woman I got and...."

The sound of the bells on the shop's door and a female calling out his name caused him to pause. Looking up from his phone, Law's eyes bucked at the sight of a familiar face. A face that he never expected to see again, a face that he'll soon to regret.

"So, you can't pick up yo phone? I know you've seen me calling, nigga. I been blowing up yo shit for the pass two weeks. "Rachel snapped, stepping in front of him, placing both hands on her hips.

Law looked her up and down like she was crazy because at that very moment, she looked as such. Rachel was a bottle girl at one of the clubs he visited frequently, and Law may have fucked her once or twice, but he was still lost as to why she was standing in front of him.

"Wad up shorty!" he hesitantly spoke, looking her up and down.

"This is what's up nigga! Happy Belated Father's Day!" Rachel shouted, stuffing a black and white ultrasound photo in his face, changing his mood for the day....... And potentially his life forever.

⁂ 9 ⁂

"**G**randma, why you and Paw Paw ain't never retire and move South like y'all said y'all would when we were kids?" Shaquita asked, taking a seat on the porch of the family building she grew up in.

"Yeah Granny. You used to always talk about building a house on the land y'all got down in Mississippi. What happened with that?" Monday chimed in before taking a lick from the vanilla ice cream cone in her hand.

It was Sunday afternoon and as promised, the girls attended church with Pastor Valentine and his First Lady. It had been about eight months since the last time Shaquita stepped foot into a church and the only reason she was present then was because it was her grandfather's anniversary. Retired for more than ten years now, they maintained a low profile but still remained active within the church.

"Well babies, we here and damn near eighty-five, we ain't got the energy to get up and move like we used to. Yo Grandad the only one who still thinks they a spring chicken and ..."

"That's because I am." Pastor Valentine interjected with the water hose in one hand and his cell phone in the other.

Both Shaquita and Monday shared a laugh at the expense of their grandparents. They loved their relationship and like every other couple in the world, they had their issues but when you're married sixty years, you seemed to get passed them.

"I'm just glad to see you girls and especially you Monday. If it wasn't for us flying to California over the years, we probably would have never seen you." Cathy voiced before standing to her feet and wiping her hands on the lavender apron she wore.

"Yeah but we blessed to have this time with y'all. So, what do you ladies have planned?" she continued, looking up the street as a man in a black leather vest and jean shorts approached the porch.

Standing to her feet to get a better view, Shaquita's eyes bucked at the sight of her Uncle June, her mother's older brother. The last time she had seen him, she was about fifteen years old and the last she heard, he was doing time for stealing out of AutoZone. Uncle June was that one family member that everyone had that just couldn't seem to get their life together. One would think that since his parents housed a church, he would have ended up on a better path but unfortunately, that wasn't the case.

"Hey Mom. Hey Dad!" Uncle June stumbled onto the concrete porch and spoke, his eyes dancing amongst everyone around him.

"And... And... Who is this? I know damn well this ain't Lil Shaq and Mo'." He smiled, showing all seven teeth in his mouth.

"Yup! That's them!" Their grandmother replied proudly from her spot near the door.

"Wooowww! Looking just like Marcia and Marsha." He began, taking a sit on the last step.

"I'm surprised to see y'all together and getting along, considering y'all mothers' relationship when they were y'all age." Uncle June looked up and stated as sweat poured from the wrinkles in his forehead.

Shaquita and Monday both locked eyes as the wheels in their heads began to spin. They knew their mothers didn't have the best sister relationship, but they always assumed it was because of the distance, but their grandparents body language told a different story.

"What you mean Unc?" Shaq chuckled lightly and asked, praying that he went on to tell his story.

"The twins were something else, they..."

"JUNE! Have you eaten anything son?" Roy, their Paw Paw, asked in a stern tone, causing both Shaquita and Monday to jump.

"Nope Pops, as a matter of fact, I..."

"It's some pork chops and rice in the house. Come on, I'll heat it up for you." Cathy cut him off and stated before turning on her heels and walking indoors with Uncle June on her trail.

Shaquita waited until the door was shut and the police sirens were gone before addressing her grandfather. It was something about the way they kept interrupting June that made her feel as if they were hiding something. The two had a close relationship and Shaq knew she'd get answers from him.

"Paw Paw, what was Uncle June talking about?" Shaq stood to her feet and asked as the sun shifted directly on her.

"Baby, you know yo Uncle June ain't himself. Those be the demons and drugs speaking for him. Don't pay him no mind." He replied from outside the gate as he continued to water the grass.

"Un huh." Monday mumbled, she too stood to her feet except this time, they prepared to leave.

Going inside the house to say their goodbyes to their grandmother, both Shaquita and Monday promised to visit in a few days as well as be in attendance for church the following Sunday. The girls enjoyed the time spent with them and knew how bless they were to still have their grandparents alive. After wrapping things up inside, the two headed back out in the heat to do the same with their Paw Paw. Making the same promises twice, the girls kissed him goodbye and left.

Once inside the car, Shaquita headed home to shower and change out of her church clothes. It was a few days before the 4th of July, and she planned on having a small BBQ in her backyard. She needed to grab a few things from Walmart such as paper plates, cups, and napkins. Law was handling the meat and anything involving grilling, therefore, she didn't have much to do herself. Passing a Buddy Bear Car Wash on the route home, Shaquita pulled inside the lot for a quick wash. Parked under a tree during service, a family of birds had a good time on the hood of her car. Thankful that it was empty, Shaquita and Monday was in and out in a matter of five minutes. Pulling inside her driveway shortly after, Shaquita prepared to kill the engine and get out when a call came through the Bluetooth in her car. Glancing at Daisy's name that flashed across, Shaq answered before making her exit.

"BITCH! You got a stalker!" Daisy's voice sounded through the speakers inside her ride, causing Shaquita to turn the volume down a few notches.

"Girl what? What is you talking about?" She turned to Monday and asked with a raised eyebrow.

"Soooooo! There's more flowers here for you AND they ain't from Law." Daisy told, peeking Shaquita's interest even more.

"So, honey listen. I'm standing outside on break with Lynette smoking a square. This nice ass truck pulls up and a fine ass nigga jump out. I'm thinking he bringing some bitch to get an abortion but instead, he walks up with some flowers. You know me, I stopped the nigga and that's when he asked if I knew you.... BITCH YOU BEEN KEEPING SECRETS? Who is that nigga?"

Shaquita's mouth flew open as Daisy continued to share the details from what took place. She had completely forgot about Weezy, especially since her and Law was back on good terms. Remembering to have only taken his number, Shaquita figured he was showing up because he didn't have another way to contact her. After telling both Monday and Daisy the story on how they met, Shaquita told Daisy that she'd call her back, she needed to reach out to her stalker. Going to the contact list in her phone, Shaq scrolled across his number and placed an outbound call to him. With the phone ringing three times, she decided to hang up just when he picked up.

"Yo." He answered in dry tone as she put the call on speaker.

"You know you can't just be coming up to my job like that." She said with firm persistence before cutting her eyes at Monday, who had a cheesy smile planted her on face.

"I can do what the fuck I wanna do... Wad up baby!" His deep voice spilled over, sending chills down her spine.

Just that quick, Shaquita remembered the face that went with the voice and got mesmerized all over again. In all truthfulness, she had forgotten about him, that happened often whenever her and Law was good. She had this thing where, she'd entertain a few niggas here and there whenever her and Law was on bad terms, but the moment, they were good, she was good. She'd cut them off, block their numbers, and completely ignore them. She was in love with Law and the fact that she'd been completely faithful their four-year bid proved that.

"Ummm.... No, the fuck you can't. What if you get me fired?" Shaquita finally shot back in a challenging tone.

"Then I'll buy you yo own clinic." Weezy assuredly replied, sending both Shaquita and Monday in cardiac arrest.

"OKAAAYYYY, MR. WEEZY! TALK YO SHIT!" Monday yelled out, filling the car with laughter from both Shaquita and him.

"Look baby, all I needed was YOUR number. I'm handling some business right now. Imma hit you back in 'bout an hour, aight." Weezy told her before ending the call and leaving both girls stuck.

❧ 10 ❧

Monday flipped through the manila folder, taking a final look at the case she'd be presenting in court next week. It was like a dream come true; since she was a kid, her only career goal was becoming an attorney. With damn near straight A's through her schooling, Monday put in the work to outshine her peers and accomplish her goals by any means necessary. Confident that her and the attorney she was working under had everything lined up perfectly in place, Monday closed the folder and put it away before preparing to leave for the day. Snatching her latest Gucci bag from out of the drawers, Monday shut down the computer system and headed out.

"Miss Valentine, can I speak to you for a second?" Mr. Hawk called out to her just as she made her way towards the elevator doors.

Unnoticeably rolling her eyes to the back of her head, Monday turned on her heels and made her way towards his office. Mr. Hawk was a partner at the firm as well as the director of the internship program she was enrolled in. Since the day she was introduced to him, he had been extremely helpful, however, it was Friday and she was more than ready to get her weekend started. In a few days, Shaquita was hosting a barbeque at her place and Monday looked forward to the activities ahead. Finally reaching his office door, she planted a fake smile on her face before stepping in.

"Good evening Mr. Hawk." She greeted him in a pleasant tone as he looked up from his MacBook Pro.

"Hey! I wanted to speak with you for a second. Close the door." He replied, his request completely catching her off guard.

Doing as he requested, Monday stepped further in and shut the door. She had no idea what they needed to discuss in private, but she'd soon learn to find out. Slamming his laptop shut, Mr. Hawk pulled his chair back and loosened the black and gray tie that hung around his neck. He had yet to utter a word, instead he smiled a creepy grin that didn't sit right with her.

"I just wanted to acknowledge your hard work and dedication over the past week. It's been a while since a law student impressed me as much as you have." He expressed behind the cherry oakwood desk.

"I also wanted to let it be known that, if you keep up the work, you'll have a spot at my law firm the minute you pass the bar." He finished.

Unsure of how to respond, Monday stood there and smiled. She appreciated his acknowledgment; however, she didn't feel like it was coming from a professional place. The entire time she's been there, Mr. Hawk, an old white man in his fifties, silently flirted with her. It was the way he smiled every time she passed him and the lustful stares she'd catch during meetings. Used to the attention from men of all ages, Monday tried her best to remain professional, she didn't have long to go.

"Thank you so much sir, I –"

"Sir? Don't call me sir, call me Harry but I mean everything I said. If you need anything.... AND I DO MEAN ANYTHING.... You let me know."

Monday's stomach turned watching the wrinkles in the corner of his eyes form from the wide smile on his face. She was beyond disgusted and couldn't believe he had the nerve to say the things that he was saying. Careful not to give off the wrong impression, Monday stood there with a blank stare on her pretty face.

"You have a good weekend and enjoy the holiday." Monday told him before doing an about-face out of his office.

Pulling her phone from her purse, Monday kicked herself in the ass the moment it died from low battery. She had a bad habit of having the charger right next to her all day but never using it until it was too late. With her irritation at an all-time high, Monday needed her phone to call an Uber, seeing how Shaq had business to take care of.

"Can you hold that elevator please?" Monday called out to the gentleman ahead of her.

Powerwalking down the long hallway, she thought about what her next move would be. She could stay a little longer and get some juice or she could catch the El-Train to Shaquita's house and prayed she arrived safely. Not being too familiar with Chicago's streets, she thought it'd be best for her to charge the phone while she was there. Stepping onto the elevator, Monday pressed the bottom that led to the cafeteria before turning around and thanking the man who held the doors for her. Doing a double take, she knew for a fact that she had to be going cray; there was no way in the world they meet up again.

"Don't I know you?" She said to him first as he stared at her biting down on his bottom lip.

"It's Wednesday, right?" He replied, chuckling lightly at his own joke.

"Very funny but you know it's Monday nigga." She smiled back, getting hypnotized and lost in his eyes.

Block was a different type of fine and Monday noticed the first time she laid eyes on him. Not easily impressed, she didn't lust over men often, but it was something about that gentleman that turned her on. She knew no one personally like him; she only read about his type in those Urban Fiction books but here he was, a book-bae, live in the flesh.

"So, this where you interning at, huh?" He stepped in closer to her and asked, his Gucci cologne captivating her nostrils.

"Yup! What you doing here?" She questioned with a raised brow.

"I was seeing my lawyer; you know Mr. Brooks he—"

"Yeah, I work with him, he's an awesome attorney, actually one of the best Criminal Defense lawyers on this side." Monday boasted on his behalf just as the elevator doors opened on her requested floor.

"Yeah, that's my nigga. What you on lunch or sum?" Block quizzed as two women joined them on the cart.

"No, I'm off. I need to charge my phone so I can call an Uber." She truthfully answered, stepping off moments before the doors began to close.

"UBER? Yo ass tweakn'... Imma drop you off." Block offered, placing his arms in between the door so she could step back in.

Without verbally responding, Monday walked back inside the elevator where she stood in front of him. Slightly feeling his dick on her ass, Monday remained still as they traveled to the lobby of the building.

"I parked in the parking lot across the street." Block announced as the two headed out the building and to his awaiting car.

"So, you like it?" She heard him ask as they made their way up the stairs to the second landing of the garage.

"It's cool. A resume builder and a few stellar recommendations ain't gon' hurt nothing." She told him as he led the way to an all-black Tesla with tinted windows.

Immediately noticing the license plates which read *"Jack Boyz1"*, Monday made a mental note to question Shaquita later about it. She talked often about Law and his crew, but Monday never found it intriguing until now. The whole bad boy, thug image was never her thing but maybe that was because she'd never been exposed to it, again..... UNTIL NOW. Popping the locks, Block headed to the passenger's side where he opened the door for her.

"Well thank you!" She grinned; her black Christian Louboutin pump entered the peanut butter interior.

"What? You shocked a nigga opened the door? Muthafucker, I got manners." Block looked down at her and smiled before shutting the door close.

Completely thrown off, Monday sat in the passenger seat like a bashful schoolgirl, cheesing. He wasn't doing things she wasn't used to but somehow and someway, she was impressed. Block's demeanor and swag screamed hood nigga and although she'd never experienced one of those, she was fairly interested now.

"Imma drop you off at the crib, let me grab something from one of my workers and then we'll head there." Block told her before turning up his music and hitting the streets.

Staring out the window, Monday watched everything in passing as they cruised the city of Chicago. Placing her phone on his charger, she replied to a few text messages and checked her social media before letting Shaquita know that she was okay. She didn't go into details but instead insured her that she was safe and on her way. Riding shotgun for a few more miles, Block finally pulled in front of an apartment building and parked. Leaving the car running, he placed a call to someone and within less than a minute, a man came running out the building towards the car.

"What's up Boss?" the young guy spoke before bending down and looking inside the car at Monday.

"What up shorty?" he spoke to her as well before directing his attention back to Block.

"I made that call and everything straight on our end... as a matter fact, I heard Chaz needed to holler at you and Law about a few things." He finished.

"You got that for me?" Block looked straight ahead and questioned, barely acknowledging anything the young man said prior.

"Yup!" he replied, pulling out a square shaped yellow manila folder and handing it to him.

"Aight. Appreciate it." Block turned to him and said before placing the stash in the glove compartment.

"Ain't you gon' count it?" The young guy curiously asked from his spot in the street.

"You niggas ain't stupid. Shut the trap down early, 12 on bullshit, I'll be back through here later." Block informed him before pulling off in the direction of Shaquita's home.

"You straight? You good? You hungry?" Block looked over at her and quizzed as he pulled to the stop sign at the corner.

"No. I'm good. Thanks for asking." She glanced at him and smiled just as his cell phone rang.

Cutting their conversation short, Block picked up the line where he had a few words back and forth with the person on the other end. After listening closely and using context clues, it was confirmed that it was Law. Tuning in even harder than before, Monday was shocked when she learned the amount of money given to him in the envelope. Impressed again for the second time that day, Monday sat back in silence the rest of the drive. Her mind was in overload and the more time she spent with Block, the more she was willing to risk it all.

❧ I I ❧

"So, who is the bitch you had in yo car on 16th yesterday?" Tisha's loud voice echoed through Block's ears the second he stepped out the shower.

Wrapping the cream and purple towel around his lower waist, he picked up his dirty clothes and walked past Tisha like she wasn't standing there. Entering the bedroom they shared for the past three years, Block went inside the drawers where he pulled out a pair of red Ethika briefs. Dropping the towel to the floor, he stepped inside the underwear and then headed to the closet.

"Aaron, you really gon' walk around here and ignore me?" Tisha followed behind him and questioned, stopping dead on his heels.

Letting out a deep sigh, Block slowly turned around and came face to face with his first love and mother of his child. Tisha was still one of the baddest to do it but his attraction to her stopped at looks. Block tried for about a year to make things work but they never seem to pull it together. He was now at a point where he needed to start making an exit plan.

"You wanna ask me about some shit that'll eventually lead into an argument. You know I'm not gon' lie to you but I'm also not about to answer a thousand questions either." He stared deep in her eyes and replied.

"Fuck all that.... WHO-WAS-IN-YO-CAR?" her hands clapped with each syllable she spoke.

Block had an obsession with honesty; he'd felt since a kid that being upfront with a person was the best way to be. Lying caused a whole bunch of extra bullshit, therefore, he only lied when he NEEDED to. Being that way was a gift and a curse, however, it was more of a curse for the person on the receiving end.

"I was dropping a homie off at the crib." He finally replied, his jawbone clenching tightly.

"Who is this homie and how you know her?" Tisha snapped, placing both hands on her hips.

"All that don't even matter. Respect the fact that I answered your question but baby momma, we ain't finna do all that extra shit." Block directly replied before turning away and getting dressed for the day.

Ignoring Tisha and her antics, Block headed out the door to pick up Law. Chaz, their supplier, called an emergency sit down meeting and neither of them knew as to why. The two had been on his payroll since they flipped their first brick. An older man in his early fifties, Chaz has been supplying the Midwest since before they were born. A cool old head, who kept a real low profile other than his name in the drug game, they didn't know much else about him. Pulling in front of Law's condo, Block shot him a text before shooting one to Chaz as well, letting him know they were headed his way. Scrolling through the CNN app on his phone, Block looked up just in time to greet Law, who was pulling open the door.

"What up Fool?"

"Shit. What up Lord!" Block spoke back before pulling away from the curb and to Chaz's crib in Naperville.

The forty-five-minute ride from out west to the suburbs consisted of the two holding various conversations while smoking two blunts. Block could tell by Law's demeanor that something was on his mind. He wasn't exactly sure what it was, however, he didn't have to wait long to find out.

"Aye, what you think this old muthafucker wanna holler at us about?" Law hit the Dutch twice and asked before releasing the smoke through his nostrils.

"Shidddd.... I don't know that but what I do know is, all our count been straight, and we been moving shit faster than ever, therefore, it can't be no complaints.... At least I don't think so." Block replied as he pulled in front of the two-story brick home.

Killing the engine, the two friends wrapped up their conversation before exiting the car and making their way towards the house. Block's eyes surveillance the area, all the while admiring everything around him. There were no police sirens in the distance. No niggas hanging on the corner and all the homes on the block shared the same manicured lawn. Chaz's house was straight out of a magazine; it was every hood niggas dream home and Block couldn't wait until he moved out the hood and started really living good. Block and his crew were hoodrich, they had the latest cars, clothes, the hottest jewelry but he always yearned for more than that. He wanted to move out the hood and raise his son somewhere where it was safe.

"Good afternoon Mr. Block and Mr. Law, Mr. Chaz is expecting you." Maria, his maid, greeted them at the door before leading them through the mansion to his den.

Navigating the same route as they have many times before, both of them silently admired the new pieces of art that hung on his wall. Chaz was heavy into the African culture and it showed by the paintings and other authentic items throughout. Finally arriving at the pinewood door, Maria knocked twice before introducing the men. Block and Law walked in and greeted Chaz with a firm handshake.

"Take a seat. Want a cigar?" He offered but they both declined.

"I hear it's about to storm something ugly so Imma jump right into it. As you both know, I look at y'all like my own sons and it's not many people I trust but I must say, y'all have earned it."

Both Block and Law listened on and smiled, nodding their heads up and down in agreement, allowing him to continue.

"In Chicago, you, along with another crew, has been handling all of my product.... Well, all that is about to change. I'm cutting the South Boys out and giving the Jack Boyz full control. There will be no more splitting, you and your team will take over 100% and everything moving forward will have to come through you two." He paused before taking a hard pull from the Cuban cigar hanging in between his fingers.

"This is going to be a major change for your entire organization. You will be coming out with 50k a week and that's on a bad week."

"DAMN!" Both Block and Law said in unison, cutting their eyes at each other.

That amount of cash on a weekly bass was a lot for two black men barely in their twenties. They already had thousands saved up and opening businesses left and right to clean dirty money and bring additional income in. Chaz's proposition was music to their ears; this is exactly the move they've been waiting for. Talking for another hour or so, Chaz filled them in on more details, putting emphasis on how much their life was getting ready to change. Leaving on a happy note, Block and Law headed back to the car where they were able to show their real excitement.

"Mannnn nigga... WHAT? Did you hear that man? We finna be checking a muthafuckn' bag!" Law excitedly barked, slapping fives with Block who prepared to pull off.

"Yeah nigga! We getting fuck'd up tonight. I ain't had no reason to celebrate lately but TONIGHT..... my nigga.... TONIGHT IS THE NIGHT!" Block assured him as he hit the expressway heading back to their side of town.

Discussing their new role inside of Chaz's organization and their new lifestyle, Block and Law were back out west before they knew it. This was the exact move he needed in order to put bigger things in play for the future. He wanted to ensure that his boy had all the things that he didn't have and thanks the Chaz, he wouldn't want for a damn thing. Preparing to merge into the right lane to make his exit, Block was stopped by Law's request.

"Man drop me off at Shaq's crib. I need to sit down and talk to her?" He uttered, causing Block to look over at him.

"You still ain't told her about shorty and the baby?" Blocked asked as he shifted directions.

"Hell naw but I know I need to before she finds out in these streets or social media." Law grimaced.

A few seconds of silence captured the car while both men became lost in their thoughts. Block knew Law was stressed out over the situation whether he'd admit it or not. A baby was something serious and knowing Shaquita, she wasn't going.

"On some real shit. What would you do?" Law asked Block, catching him completely off guard.

"On some real shit. I'll make that bitch kill it....."

"I tried. Even offered her some bread.... She ain't budging." Law reluctantly reported.

"Then kill her. If I was bogus... LIKE YOU.... And I know for a fact I ain't trying to lose my girl... Then I'll off the bitch that's causing the problem but then again.... That's how I'm riding for mine." Block truthfully told his best friend as he pulled in front of Shaquita's crib.

"And speaking of mine....Is Monday up there?" Block killed the engine and asked; however, he was out the car and going to see for himself before Law could even reply.

❧   12   ❧

Placing his key inside the door, Law prepared to tell his girl the truth and prayed that he didn't lose her forever. Block was right about everything he had stated, but Law wasn't the type to take a life simply because he fucked up. Rachel and everything dealing with her were a mistake that he would most likely regret for the rest of his life. After she attacked him with the pregnancy news a few days back, Law did all he could do to convince her to get an abortion. He tried talking sense into her, he even offered to pay her off, however, nothing seemed to work. Just like every other girl in the hood, they dreamed of trapping a Jack Boy, with hopes of making a come up, but Law refused to be anyone's puppet. He loved Shaquita and although he didn't want to lose her, he still needed to come clean.

"The fuck y'all doing in here?" He walked in unannounced and asked, startling both Shaquita and Monday. who sat at the kitchen counter on a laptop.

"Ummmm... I live here and how did you get yo key back?" Shaquita looked up and questioned, staring both Law and Block down.

"I stole it back the first time I came over. What y'all looking at?" He quizzed, walking over to where they were seated.

"I should've known." He chuckled to himself while they drooled over the latest collection of Louie Vuitton purses.

Making his way over to the stainless-steel refrigerator, Law opened it up and grabbed two cold bottles of Aquafina water. Tossing one over the girl's head at Block, who caught it like a receiver on the field. Cracking open the top, Law took a swig from the bottle, emptying it with one gulp.

"Don't be throwing shit in my shit." Shaquita snapped, her head twisting in both men direction.

"And what the hell y'all doing over here anyway?" Shaq continued from her spot at the kitchen counter.

"I came to talk to you and ..."

"I came over here to see Monday." Block cut Law off and chimed in, putting a huge smile on Monday's face.

"See! NOPE! Get the fuck out... BYE BLOCK!" Shaq jumped up and yelled, playfully escorting him to the door.

"Mannnnn Shaq, chill. Imma treat her right." Block laughed while him and Monday stared intensely at each other.

Law laughed at the exchange between his best friend and girl and knew this was only the beginning. Although Law didn't know Monday personally, he been around Shaquita for years and knew how close the two was. From what he could tell, she was spoiled, and Law knew that she wasn't used to a nigga like Block. Block was a different breed and maybe Shaquita was doing right by keeping her away.

"Mannnn leave them alone and let me holler at you in the bedroom." Law grabbed her by the arm and called out, pulling her away, leaving Block and Monday by themselves.

Law held onto Shaq's hand as they walked up the stairs and to her bedroom. He tried rehearsing in his head, the ways the conversation could take place. He was more scared than he ever been. He felt like Usher in his song *Confessions*, how was he supposed to tell the woman he loved that he was having a baby by a woman he barely even knew? Shaquita wasn't the type to stick around and with all of Law's doing in the past, he couldn't blame her.

"What? What's wrong?" She walked in and asked, her eyes searching his as he closed the bedroom door behind her.

"Why you think something wrong?" He looked her in the eyes and asked, wondering if she had heard something already and just wanted him to come clean first.

"Nigga, I know you. Now tell me. What's wrong?" Shaquita walked up closer to him and quizzed, staring up at him.

Law took one look in her eyes and folded. There was no way in the world he could break her heart again, especially after all those times he promised not to. Law knew the type of woman he had and although he hadn't shown it in the past, he really wasn't trying to lose her.

"Me and Block just came from seeing Chaz and he promoted us, giving us full control over Chicago's product." He told her as he forced a smile on his face.

"Oh my God baby, that's great! I'm happy for y'all and y'all been working hard for this shit!" she cheered on before wrapping her arms around his neck, hugging him tightly.

Law lifted Shaq off the floor and wrapped her legs around his waist. Placing soft kisses on his neck, Shaq congratulated him over and over again. Both her body and words caused his dick to rise in his jeans and they both knew what that meant. Slowly walking her over to the bed, Law brought Shaquita's mouth to his and kissed her passionately. Placing her down lightly on the bed, he wasted no time pulling her shorts to the side and diving in. Law sucked her pussy like it was his last meal and he had something to prove.

"Damn.... What the fuck bae?" Shaq lifted her head and moaned, causing Law's eyes to travel to hers.

"You finna make meeeeeee......"

Shaquita's words were cut short by the sound of Law slurping on her clit, sending her body into overdrive. Her legs shook uncontrollably as she came again. Coming up for air, Law locked eyes with his girl before licking her juices off his lips and signaling for her to come out of her shorts. Doing as she was told, Shaquita pulled them off quickly while Law did the same.

"Bend over." He ordered and just like before, she obeyed.

Once they both were positioned and ready to go, Law slid his thick dick inside of her and went to work, hitting all his favorite spots. Between her wet pussy and her soft moans, Law was ready to explode in a matter of minutes. Gripping her waist, he picked up his speed and so did she.

"I'm finna cum... WATCH OUT!." He warned, preparing to pull out and shoot on her ass.

"No! No! Keep it in...." She moaned loudly, letting him know she was cumming as well.

"I ain't got on no condom baby..... Fuckkkkk!' Law grunted, feeling his nut building at the tip of his dick.

"Cum in me! Cum in me! I'm ready for your babies. I love you Law. I love youuuuu....." Shaquita screamed out in ecstasy, shooting his seed inside of her and making things way much more complicated than they already were.

$$\text{❈} \quad 1\,3 \quad \text{❈}$$

"Okay.... So, we got the paper plates, napkins, cups, tablecloths, and lighter fluid. Yup! That was the last thing." Shaquita noted as her eyes scrolled the handmade list she held in her hand.

They had been inside Walmart for almost twenty minutes getting the final items on the list. It was Independence Day and due to them being last minute, they were stuck in a long line at nine o'clock in the morning. Stepping up a few feet while things moved along, Shaquita thought about the other errands she had to run just as her phone vibrated in her hands.

"What the fuck....This like the thirty-seventh time today." She cursed, looking down at the private call on her screen.

On top of waking up to several private calls, they hadn't stopped yet and it was starting to piss Shaquita off. The number she had was fairly new and she hadn't had someone play on her phone since high school. Ignoring the call and placing her items on the belt, the phone vibrated again, this time, Shaquita answered it.

"Who the fuck is this?" She snapped while a female's voice on the other end giggled before ending the call in her face.

"They say something?" Monday quizzed with a puzzled expression.

"Nope but the bitch laughed. Who the fuck calls somebody phone just to laugh?" Shaquita rhetorically questioned before speaking to the cashier in front of her.

"I ain't know bitches still played on phones." Monday shrugged while Shaquita's mind began to race.

"Thank you ma'am," She said to the cashier before grabbing her receipt and pushing the cart forward.

"I bet it's one of Law's hoes.... Ohhhh!! I swear to God, I'll bet my last that it's one of his bitches playing on my line." Shaq continued as they walked out the door and into the hot sun.

"Cousin, don't jump to no conclusions now. I don't think Law would mess around with a childish ass female that'll play on phones. Maybe they got the wrong number and think you somebody else. You only had this number for a few months." Monday reminded her as the girls placed the bags in the trunk along with fireworks and some other things.

Letting Monday's words resonate in her head, she prayed like hell her favorite cousin was right. Outside of the incident on Facebook, she hadn't had any issues with Law for months prior. Shaquita knew her nigga like she knew the back of her hand and although he was no saint, she knew Law loved her.

"Monday, as God is my witness, if I hear ANYTHING about this nigga and him being dirty.... I'm DONE! On my kids I'm done with that nigga." Shaquita looked over at Monday and assured her.

"And since when you become Team Law?" She continued and asked with a smirk on her face.

"I'm not team Law.... I'm not team nobody but ...."

"And you only saying this shit cuz you wanna keep Block around.... Bitch you ain't slick." Shaquita cut her off and stated between giggles.

"Girl! No! No! And no! I ain't checking for that nigga. I mean, he's fine as fuck and all but I'm damn near married and Martin is a million-aire in the making. What the hell a Jack Boy gon' do for me?" Monday told her as they pulled into the parking lot of Binny's.

"Yeah! Yeah! Yeah! I hear you but don't sleep on those Jack Boyz sis. Those niggas sum hood millionaires." Shaquita fact checked before killing the engine and hopping out.

Walking into the air-conditioned establishment, both girls' eyes scanned the store briefly before heading over to the Vodka section. Scrolling each aisle, the girls grabbed what they needed and what they didn't need before making their way to the counter. With the cart full, both Shaquita and Monday began placing the bottles on the belt. Patron, Henny, and Don Julio were their pick with their total nearing seven-hundred dollars. A few guys entered the store, trying to get their attention, helped out by placing the liquor in the car for them. After thanking them and sending them about their way, Shaquita then headed to her final stop.

"I gotta open the gate at my momma's house for Uncle June. He's cutting the grass for her whiles she's away in Brazil." Shaq filled Monday in on their next adventure.

Arriving at her mom's house less than fifteen minutes later, Shaquita grabbed her set of keys and left Monday in the car. Looking up and down the street for Uncle June, Shaq retreated inside the house with hopes of escaping the heat. Snatching up the mail, Shaquita walked in the lien scented house and damn near fell out. Cursing at her mom for not leaving the windows crack, Shaq walked through the house and did it herself. After doing a final walk through to ensure everything was intact, she headed back out the door, running into Uncle June, who walked up the steps.

"Hey Uncle June. How are you?" Shaq asked, using her hands to cover her eyes with attempts to block the sun.

"I'm good baby girl. Ready to take care of this lawn for my baby sister so I can go eat." Uncle June replied, wiping the stream of sweat that fell from his forehead.

"Okay, well be safe. The water hose in the back. She said you was watering those ugly ass plants too. Here's twenty Unc. See you later." Shaquita said to him before leaving out the gate and across the street to her car.

Waiting for the vehicles to pass, Shaq thought she heard Uncle June call out to her from the porch. Turning around to make sure, she waited for a U-Haul truck to pass when he called out again, confirming her thoughts. With the sun in her way, Shaquita squinted her eyes before replying.

"What's up Uncle June?" she yelled out loudly over the traffic noise.

"I seen yo daddy the other day. I ain't seen him since before I got locked up." Uncle June yelled back out to her but she knew for a fact she had to be hearing him wrong.

"What was that Uncle June?" Shaquita screamed just as her phone vibrated in her hands.

Looking down at the screen, she stared at the unsaved number and wondered to herself where she had seen it from before. Digging deep in her thoughts, she finally recognized the number, it belonged to Weezy. She hadn't spoken to him since she was tricked into giving him her number and although she looked forward to the call, now was bad timing.

"UNCLE JUNE! WHAT YOU SAY?" Shaq howled; however, it was useless, he was nowhere to be found.

Hesitantly making her way to the car, Shaquita looked around with hopes of seeing where he disappeared to. She thought about going back over there to find him but decided not to. It was almost noon and they needed to start prepping for the barbeque before her guest arrived. Opening the door, Shaquita joined Monday inside the cool car. Shifting the gears to drive, Shaq kept her foot on the break and stared across the street at her mother's home. Totally lost in thought, she hadn't heard Monday call out to her until it was too late.

"Girl, is you okay?" She tapped her and asked, fully snapping her out of her daze.

"Yeah... Yeah.... I'm good.... Uncle June just said something that had me confused." Shaquita admitted, pulling Monday's face from her phone.

"What he say?" Monday looked at her and asked.

"He said.... He said he seen my dad........but ghee...... my daddy's dead...." Shaquita replied, causing Monday's mouth to drop.

❧ 14 ☙

"I don't know how creditable Uncle June is Shaquita.... Think about it, the man been in jail since we were kids and he's still heavy on the drugs. I'm pretty sure he was high or something and seen someone who looks like your father." Monday said from the stove while she stirred the bake beans in the pot.

"I get all that, but he also said that he hadn't seen him since before he got locked up. Uncle June went to jail when I was ten and my Daddy died while my mother was pregnant with me, so, high or not, the timeframe still doesn't make sense."

Monday watched as her cousin prepared the potato salad, thinking about the current conversation they were having. Shaquita's energy shifted the moment she got back in the car, even placing a call to her mom with questions but Aunt Marsha didn't pick up. Monday hated that Shaq was feeling this way, especially on a day like today.

"Listen, don't worry about that shit cuzn, everything good, we about to enjoy ourselves. As a matter of fact... HERE!" Monday stated before sliding a bottle of Patron across the counter.

"Pour both of us a shot." Monday continued telling her as Shaq did what she requested.

Turning the stove on low, Monday stirred her famous baked beans one last time before placing the lid on top. Turning around on her heels, Monday wiped her hands on the apron she wore before joining Shaquita at the kitchen counter.

"Let's go baby!" Shaq held her glass in the air and yelled, causing Monday to smile.

"Aye bitches. Wait on me!" Daisy walked in from the backyard and interrupted, stopping them in their tracks.

"Come on friend. Here!" Shaq turned to her and replied, pouring her a shot glass as well.

The girls went three rounds before turning up the music and finish prepping. Having control over the sides, Law and Block was on their way over to start the meats. The thought of Block or even hearing his name made Monday feel some type of way. The other day when Shaquita and Law left them alone to fuck, the two of them held one of the best conversations she'd ever had in her life. Learning about him, his childhood, his son, and the other important things in his life made Monday feel a weird connection to him. The physical attraction was a given, but it was something else, something different, something she couldn't explain. The hour conversation they held was deep and Monday hadn't stopped thinking about him since he left.

"The beans done, I'm about to hop in the shower, y'all." Monday announced, removing the lavender apron and placing it on the stool.

"Yeah me too. Imma take the bathroom downstairs." Daisy chimed in, heading towards the lower level of Shaquita's duplex.

"A bitch gotta smell good for Block!" she yelled out before she hit the stairs, sending stares in her direction.

"I know you ain't gon' let her take yo man." Shaq joked before heading up to her bedroom while Monday went towards hers.

"You sound stupid.... That ain't my man and if he was, Daisy couldn't take shit." Monday cockily boasted, speaking loud enough so Daisy could hear.

Showering and washing her hair, Monday settled on a simple wash and go look for the day, tossing on a pair of Fashion Nova shorts with the crop top to match. It was almost 100 degrees out which meant being cute wasn't an option. After applying lotion and perfecting her baby hairs, Monday headed out the bedroom door just as Shaquita made her way to answer the front door.

"What the fuck you steal a key for if you gon' still ring the bell?"

"Shut up. This shit heavy....Move!" Monday heard Law's voice say followed by him and Block walking past them with bags of ice, coolers, meat, and other things.

"What's up beautiful?" Block stopped in front of Monday and spoke before heading out the backyard door.

"Heyyyyy Block" Daisy appeared out of nowhere and spoke, batting her eyelashes.

"What up shorty? Aye Shaq, where you want me to put this?" Block asked, referring to the case of Don Julio he carried.

"We got enough liquor honestly. You can put it on the patio though." She instructed while the girls headed to the kitchen.

Mixing up a few drinks inside while the guys went right to work out on the grill out back, Monday couldn't stop thinking about how good Block looked. She wasn't sure if it was the drinks they kept knocking back, but she had never met someone so sexy.

"Oh shit! This Martin. I'll be back." Monday said to the girls before taking off in the room to answer his call.

Locking eyes with Block who walked in just as she disappeared, Monday entered the bedroom and closed the door behind her. Flopping down on the bed, Monday kicked off her flip flops and laid back. Her room seemed to be the coolest in the house and she was enjoying every moment of it.

"Hey babyyyyyy!" She finally placed the phone to her ear and sang while a huge smile invaded her face.

"I miss you so much sweetie." Martin's calm voice spoke from the other end, making her smile even more.

"I miss you too and can't wait until September so I can come home to you." Monday replied, standing to her feet and walking over towards the window in the room.

"Well actually, that's why I was calling. Our trip was cut short and I'm leaving tomorrow. I was thinking about catching a flight straight there. Baby, I can't wait all the way until September to see you." Martin expressed.

"Ummmm, bae.... As much as I wanna see you, I don't wanna inconvenience anyone. I know you're tired and your granny has been sick. You don't have to come baby, I ---"

"This is my dad, Monday. I'll call you back." He cut her off in mid-sentence and stated before ending the call in her face.

Shrugging her shoulders, Monday headed back over to the door just as there was a knock on it.

"Come in." she yelled out, looking down, sliding back on her shoes.

"Girl, tell me why Martin's ass...." Monday began to say to Shaquita but stopped when she realized that it wasn't her at the door.

"What you in here doing when you supposed to be out here with me?" Block walked in and questioned, shutting the door behind him.

"I – I- I was just on my way back out. Come on." She said, trying to slip pass him but was stopped by his broad shoulders and muscular body.

"Nah.... I'm good now. We can chill in here." He replied in a low tone, walking deeper into the bedroom.

"Huh? I'm lost. Chill in here? What you want?" she questioned shyly, feeling intimated yet turned on.

"You." He stepped in closer to her and uttered.

"I want you." Block repeated as he towered over her small frame.

"But – But Block, I got a man." Monday truthfully spoke but her words only drew him in more.

"Fuck that nigga. He ain't me. Come here." He ordered, pulling her by the arms towards him.

Block took his lips and placed them on hers, instantly filling her golden skin with goosebumps. She had never in her life been kissed the way that man was kissing her right then and there. As much as she thought she wanted to pull away, she couldn't. Monday, for some reason, couldn't resist Block but then again, she wasn't really trying.

"Take these off." He told her in between kisses while she followed his order.

Sliding out the shorts she just placed on, a wave of emotions set over her as she tried to figure out what exactly she was doing. She had only had sex with Martin, and it took him a year to get some, yet, here she was, fucking a man she didn't know. It was like Block knew voodoo and had control over her doll, the way he managed to make her body feel in ways she never knew it could feel. Sliding inside her, it felt as if he was ripping her insides but in a slow pleasuring way. Sex with Martin didn't feel nearly as good as it did with Block. After bending her over and hitting her with a few teasers from the back, Block tapped her on the ass and told her to turn around.

"You way too fine to be fucked from behind." He looked her in the eyes and said as she scooted back on the bed.

Spreading her legs apart, Monday watched as Block took a step back and licked his lips. He was turning her on something crazy and he had no idea. The sight of him alone made her pussy throb and she wanted nothing more than his dick back inside of her.

"Block…. Stop playing with me." She spoke out to him in a low flirtatious tone, motioning him towards her with her short-manicured nails.

Obedient, Block followed her instructions but instead of dicking her down, he dove in, headfirst. The second the tip of his tongue touched her already swollen clit, Monday felt like exploding. Block engaged in a passionate tongue twisting match with her pussy, defeating her and her body in two minutes.

"I ain't done. Gimmie a kiss." He brought his head up and told her, sliding his dick back inside while their tongues danced around in each other's mouth.

Monday's body went through some things she could never explain. Experiencing her first orgasm, it was everything she thought it would be, just not from the person who she thought it would be with. Monday loved Martin; she knew for a fact but now, Block had her doubting that.

❧   15   ❧

L aw placed the pack of pencils along with the spiral bond notebook inside the navy-blue backpack and passed it to the kid behind him.

"Here you go lil man, now go over there and holler at my girl, she'll make you and yo homies some plates." Law instructed the snag tooth kid before sending him in Shaquita's direction.

It was the Jack Boyz's annual back to school block party and just like the previous four years, it was a success. Every year, Law and his crew organized a huge block party for the kids in the neighborhood. Handing out school supplies, they also barbequed and held other fun activities for the entire family to enjoy. This was one day where everyone who grew up in the hood came back and chilled with old familiar faces.

"Aight, that was the last shorty. Help me put the rim up so I can bust y'all ass in some ball." Law heard Block say from behind him, causing him to chuckle and shake his head.

"Nigga, that's cuz you big as fuck. Ain't nobody trying to guard you."

"Naw nigga, that's cuz CAN'T none of you niggas guard me." Block flexed showing off his muscles in the white wife beater he wore.

Ignoring Block and his capping, Law turned around just as Shaquita and Monday walked up. It had been two weeks since the fourth and he still hadn't managed to come clean about Rachel and the pregnancy. Coming up with different ways every day to tell her, he couldn't stand breaking her heart again.

"We done passing out the food baby." Shaq appeared in front of him, standing on her tippy toes and placing a kiss on his cheeks.

"Cool. I'm about to hoop real quick and fuck up these kids in a water balloon fight then it should be time to close up shop." Law replied.

"Ok and in the meantime, me and Monday will be over here tagging they ass in some double dutch." Shaq told him before tugging at her arm.

"Nah...... Monday need to go take them lil ass shorts off." Block barked as the two stared each other down.

Since Block hit, him and Monday had been inseparable, practically glued at the hip. She was all his homie talked about, which was weird because Law wasn't used to hearing it. Block had hoes left and right, but the man never caught feelings. Somehow, him and Tisha ended up trying to work things out, which never seemed to work out. Monday was the first chick he had ever seen have his best friend's nose open. On top of her not living in Chicago AND having a nigga, Law wasn't sure Block was doing a smart thing.

"Her boyfriend gon' fly here and beat yo ass." Law joked, breaking the silence amongst them as the girls walked away.

"I'll shoot buddy's ass, but nigga don't worry about me, worry about Rachel and that baby shower y'all finna be planning." Block shot back, hitting Law where it hurt.

"Too soon nigga .... Too soon.... But anyway, Lil Dee was telling me he heard about some niggas on Facebook from out south who supposed to be coming to holler at us." Law reported as the two headed to the other end of the block.

"Yeah, nigga said some shit to me at the car wash about it yesterday. Supposedly, some nigga name Weezy run the land and got a problem with us cuz Chaz took food off their plate and put it on ours." Block explained while they set the basketball rim up.

"Weezy? Weezy? Imma look into that but ....."
BANG! BANG! BANG! BANG! BANG!

Five shots rang out, by the second one, Law hit the ground. He could feel his leg burning but instead of attending to that, he and Block fired back. Screams and cries from women and babies filled his ears as he struggled to stand to his feet.

"OH MY GOD BABY... DON'T MOVE! YOU'VE BEEN SHOT!" Shaquita wept, kneeling down to his aid while Block checked on Monday.

"EVERYBODY IN THE FUCKN' HOUSE....NOW!" Block's deep voice roared through the streets.

Everyone ran for shelter while half of their crew chased the car who came through spraying. He couldn't believe the audacity of niggas and little did they know, they'd started a war. It had been a few years since anyone tried the Jack Boyz; they had made their mark in the streets and was fairly respected. Law knew for a fact it was some out south hoes that were behind the trigger.

"Shaquita, bring yo car around and take Law to Mt. Sinai. Monday, get in the car with them. I'll be up there as soon as I make sure everyone else on our end is good." Block stated while helping him to his feet.

Shaquita and Monday ran off and did as they were told while the guys secured the area. It took them about three minutes to get through with the car and the pain in his leg was worsening. Thankful because he knew it could had been worst, Law limped over to the car and got in. Monday drove while Shaquita gave directions and inspected his wombs from the backseat. Thankful again, this time because his girl was a nurse. Law tossed his head back and closed his eyes until they arrived. Entering the emergency room where they checked to see if the bullet was still present, after discovering that it was not, they sent him back out to the waiting area.

"Block just text me and said he's on his way." Monday looked up from her phone and reported.

The three sat around talking and watching Jerry Springer on the small box tv mounted on the wall. Block must have been closer than they thought because he came walking through the hospital doors five minutes later. Taking a seat next to Monday, he pulled her in a hug before kissing her on the forehead. Law had completely forgotten about her and being out of her element. Shaquita's been around, therefore she knew the life that came with it, but Monday, she seemed sheltered and shaken up.

"What they saying?" Block quizzed while Monday held on to him tight.

"Shit.... I'm waiting on they ass to patch me up and send me home." Law replied, pulling his ringing phone from his pocket.

Sitting around another thirty minutes or so, Block made the girls go home and change since they had blood on them. Block must have been his guardian angel because the second Shaquita and Monday walked out, Rachel and one of her home girls walked in.

"Oh my God, are you okay? I came as soon as I heard about what happened." She walked towards him and exclaimed, taking a seat in Shaquita's chair.

"Damn girl, this yo baby daddy?" Her homie smirked, causing both Law and Block's eyes to dart in her direction.

"Why you here?" Law bluntly asked, snatching his arm away from her.

"What you mean? You the father of my baby and...." She paused, standing to her feet and rubbing her flat belly.

"I gotta make sure you good." She finished, flopping back down in the cushioned chair.

Letting out a deep sigh while Block laughed like he was at a Kevin Hart show, Law placed his face inside the palm of both hands. He had just dodged a bullet, but he wasn't so sure how much more luck he'd have. He hadn't heard from Rachel in a few days and here she was showing up at the wrong time. Law knew if he wanted to keep his girl then he might have to take Block's advice after all.

❧ 16 ❧

If them bitches 'round you, better be blood
   If it ain't me or your mama, shouldn't be showin' you no love
   Please forgive me, I know that I'm stingy
'Cause baby I'm gang 'bout you
Ain't playing no games 'bout you
I'll go to hell and jail 'bout you boy
I'll go to hell and jail about you boy

Shaquita's hip swayed side to side to the sweet sounds of Summer Walker as she flipped yet another successful pancake. Despite her man being shot a few days ago, Shaquita was in a good mood. It was something about the way the sun shined that made her wanna cook the entire house breakfast. Law dicked her down with one leg about thirty minutes ago, adding to the positive mood she was already in. After stirring the cheese grits on the stove, she then turned off the eye that cooked the sausage.

"Damn! A bitch in a good mood I see." Shaq heard Monday say, causing her to mute the music coming from her Airpods.

"Is that nigga still in my house?" Shaq asked, pointing to Monday's bedroom door while she slid across the kitchen towards her.

"Noooo! Ugh! Don't hug me. You probably just got done sucking dick." Shaquita said, twisting and turning while Monday pulled her into a bear hug.

"Good morning cousin. What you cooking?" Monday released her grip and questioned while she searched the pots on the stove.

"FOOD! Now move." Shaq fussed, pushing Monday out her way so she could finish up.

Grabbing the plates out of the cabinets, Shaquita prepared breakfast while Monday sat at the kitchen counter with her face buried in her phone. She was really enjoying her cousin's company and knew it was going to break her heart seeing her leave. Monday was holding things down at work and although she thought Block would be a distraction, he had actually been motivation. He made sure Monday got her ass up for work no matter what they got into the night before. He was truly making her happy but the two were playing a dangerous game.

"I wonder what the fuck he be telling Tisha?" Shaquita blurted out, catching Monday off guard.

"What the fuck you mean?" She asked defensively with a screwed-up face.

"Chill baby!" Shaq giggled, placing both hands in the air like she was surrendering.

"What I mean is..... He's clearly still involved with his baby mother because they live together. And if I'm her.... I ain't going. The nigga ain't been home in 'bout three days and then YOU.... You done forgot about poor little Martin. Fucking Block in bathrooms and cars and shit." Shaquita preached while Monday struggled to keep a straight face.

She meant everything she said to her little cousin, however and most importantly, she didn't want to see Monday hurt. She'd been knowing Block for years and knew the type of nigga he was. Shaquita had seen him with several women in the past but no matter what, he always went back to Tisha. She seemed to have his heart and Monday wasn't snatching that.

"The food ready?" Law appeared, limping down the stairs with a cane in his hand and questioned.

"Yeah, I was just about to call you. Monday grab Block so his free loading ass can come eat too." Shaquita replied before heading to the stove to make the plates.

Once everyone was settled and seated, they dug in, filling their stomachs with pancakes, grits, sausage, and eggs. Shaquita put her foot in that breakfast and from the looks at everyone plates, they agreed. Monday stayed behind to help clean while the men got dressed and left, handling business per usual. After wrapping things up in the kitchen, Shaquita headed upstairs to shower and dress as well. She had a couple errands to run and with her vacation coming to an end, she wanted to relax as much as possible. Turning on her blue tooth speaker, she sat her phone on the charger nearby and entered the bathroom. Washing up and drying in a matter of ten minutes, Shaquita was placing her hair in a high bun and heading out the door.

"You wanna ride with me?" She stopped at the couch and asked Monday who lounged around on it.

"Nope! Block on his way back to get me. He's taking me to the gun range." Monday lifted her head and replied.

After exchanging a few more words, Shaquita was out the door and on her way to the nail shop. Stopping off at the bank first, she then made her way to the gas station where she filled her tank up. Ignoring the perverted stares and disrespectful chants, Shaquita jumped back in the car and pulled off. Making a right on the next block, Shaquita did a double take when she spotted Uncle June walking towards the liquor store. Pulling over and jumping out, Shaquita called out his name three times before he finally turned around and acknowledge her.

"Lil Shaq, that's you?" He asked, struggling to see and walk straight.

"Gimmie three dollars." His words slurred while she went in her back pocket and pulled out a twenty.

"Thank you niece. Thank you!" He gracefully accepted the cash before turning and walking away.

"Uncle June... WAIT! I gotta question." Shaquita called out again, stopping him in his tracks like before.

Ray Charles could see that Uncle June was as high as a kite and Shaq was starting to feel bad about giving him the money, feeding to his addiction. At the time, she wasn't thinking straight. She had been trying to catch up with Uncle June since the day she seen him at her mother's house. Her mom broke her phone while out of the country with her friends and Shaquita hadn't been able to talk to her yet. Every day she thought about what Uncle June said to her and now she was finally able to get clarification.

"Last time I seen you, you said you saw my daddy.... Where you see him at?" Shaquita quizzed, stepping in closer so she could hear him clearly.

"I seen him at the gas station on Independence." Uncle June replied, keeping it short.

"Are you sure it was MY dad?" Shaq questioned, anxious to hear his answer.

"I'm positive. I know Billy when I see him." He looked up the street nervously and told her.

Letting out a deep sigh, Shaquita felt like a weight had been lifted off her shoulders. Uncle June was high and out of his mind and it was good to know that she had been tripping for no reason. Her father name wasn't Billy, Uncle June was definitely mistaking.

"My daddy named Montel, Uncle June.... Not Billy." Shaquita explained to him, shifting her weight to one side, trying to avoid the sun.

"I was around before you. I think I'll know who yo Daddy is. Montel was your mother's best friend, he passed away before you were born.... He may be your God-Daddy, but I know who yo real daddy is.... Hell, I used to work for him." Uncle June chuckled before taking off down the street at the sound of his name.

"UNCLE JUNE, STOP!" Shaq screamed, reaching forward, pulling him back by the dingy white tee he wore.

"I need you to pay attention right now. Them other hypes can wait. What more do you know about Billy?"

"I just came home. I don't know much of shit...... He did tell me if I needed a job, I can come work at one of his restaurants." Uncle June finally focused and explained.

"What's the name of his restaurant?" Shaq asked while she still had his attention.

"It's a new soul food place on Madison, you should go check it out." He suggested before skipping away down the street with his friends.

Confused more than ever, Shaquita began to question everything she'd ever been told. Although Uncle June was high as giraffe pussy, he didn't pull that story from his ass. Shaquita had always been told that her father died in a car accident before she was born. Never asking too many questions, Shaq had always been satisfied with that story, until now.

Jumping back in the car, Shaquita headed to her grandparents' house where she searched for more answers. She knew they knew more than anybody, Shaq just prayed they kept it one hundred with her. Pulling up in front of their house five minutes later, Shaquita killed the engine and grabbed her phone to let them know she was out front. With no answer from either of their cells or the house phone, she thought it would be best to stay put, she knew they'd call back. Trying to take her mind off of things, Shaquita surfed through her social media accounts, finishing off with Snapchat. Looking at a few stories, she stopped at a new friend, some chick name Rachel, she accepted at few days ago. Tapping through her story, Shaquita's heart dropped in her stomach when she came across a video of Law in the hospital waiting room. Looking at the date stamp on the video, it was uploaded from her camera roll, which meant, she recorded the video the day he was shot. With her eyes now zooming in on the caption, Shaquita saw nothing but red:

"Had To Make Sure Daddy Was Good"

With her phone still in hand, Shaquita went to Law's name in her contact list and placed a call, but lucky for him, he didn't answer. Starting her car back up, Shaq planned on hitting all the spots she knew he frequent at. She wanted to make sure Law didn't see what he had coming. Shifting the gear into drive, Shaq prepared to pull out when her phone rang. Not even paying attention to the number, she hit the button on her sterling wheel, connecting the calls.

"HELLO!" She snapped aggressively at the caller on the other end.

"Damn, you good?" A familiar voice filled her car and asked, causing her to look at the name on her screen.

It seemed like Weezy had the worst timing when it came to calling. He always caught her at a bad moment, like when she was in a bad mood or when Law was around. Not wanting to take her anger out on him, Shaquita decided to switch it up a little.

"My bad. I'm good. Where you at?" She asked him, pulling away from the curb and into the flow of traffic.

"Ummmm... I'm around. What's up?" he replied and she could tell he was caught off guard by is tone.

"I'm trying to see you tonight. Let's get a room."

Shaquita's words surprised even herself, however, she was done playing games with Law and if he wanted to have bitches, then may the best dog win.

❧ 17 ❧

“Fucckkkk Block... Oh My Godddddd! I'm --- I'm ---- I'm cumnnnnn," Monday tilted her head back and screamed out as Block dug his nails in her waist.

Feeling his dick pulsate inside of her, Mo' knew he was reaching his peek as well, so she stayed up there a little longer. Gripping her pussy muscles, she smiled while staring in his eyes; Block had her dickmatized and he ain't even know it. Slowly sliding off top, Monday laid on his tatt'd chest while he placed kisses on the top of her head.

"You good baby?" His deep voice echoed through the room, sending chills all over her body.

"I'm good. Why you ask?" She titled her head upwards towards him and quizzed.

"Imma ask that a few times a day. That's just some shit you'll have to get used to, but, you've been a little different since the block party. I know you shaken up after the shootout but you gotta understand this, that type of shit, happens when you fuck with a nigga like me, but more so, you'll never have to worry about shit, fucking with a nigga like me. I'm yo protector and whether you near or far, Imma protect you." Block sat up and explained, his words causing more chills to form on her body.

Monday wasn't sure how to explain the feelings she had for Block, but it was something deep. She was one-hundred percent sure Martin was the one she'd marry, now, she wasn't so sure. Block had her looking at life different, he made her feel like a different woman, all the while living at home with another woman. Monday tried her best not the think about Block and Tisha, but she couldn't help it. Block assured her all the time that him and his baby mother were over and done with, however, something inside herself said elsewise. How much could Monday really trip? She had a man at home and wasn't in a position to talk.

"Let me get up for work." She finally sat up and stated, placing two soft pecks on his lips.

Heading into the bathroom, Monday relieved herself on the toilet first before handling her hygiene at the sink. Stepping inside the steamy shower and washing over her body twice, Monday rinsed off her favorite Dove Lavender bodywash and jumped out. Grabbing the yellow towel off the rack, she wrapped it around her tightly before stepping out.

"Okay, Mrs. Parker. I understand and I apologize. I'll be there in twenty." Block said before looking up at her and ending the call.

"What's wrong? Everything okay?" She asked, dropping the towel and moving about the room.

"Tisha's ole goofass ain't pick my son up from her mother's house and now Mrs. Parker late for work. Hoe ain't answering her phone or nun." Block replied as he dialed her number over and over.

"Get up and finish getting dressed so you can go get the baby. I'll have Shaq drop me off at work." Shaquita told him while she dressed in a black pencil skirt and white blouse.

"Nah, I just text Law, he about to swing by and get me. Here.... Take my car and keep it until you leave. I got two more at the crib. You don't need to be depending on nobody to get around and that Uber and Lyft shit dead." Block stood to his feet and replied, leaving her speechless.

"Ummmm Ok- Okay. I'll call you on my lunch." Monday told him before taking the keys and standing on her tippy toes, kissing him on his lips.

Grabbing her briefcase and purse, Monday headed out the door and to Block's black Telsa, where she plugged in the address and headed to work. One would think she knew the area by heart, but one would be wrong. She had a horrible sense of direction and Chicago's streets were something else. Stopping off at Starbucks along the way, Monday hit the drive thru and ordered a large hazelnut coffee. Satisfied with the taste, she pulled off and made her way into the office. With Block and his dick fresh on her mind, Monday was in the best mood and it had been that way lately.

"Good morning Miss Valentine, can I see you in my office please?" Mr. Hawk peeked his head out the door and requested.

Feeling like she spoke too soon, Monday changed directions, entering the brightly lit high-rise office. The breathtaking view from the nineteenth floor helped with the fake smile she managed to plaster on her face. All she wanted to do was her six hours and clock out so she could go be under Block.

"Good morning Mr. Hawk. How can I help you?" She asked, making sure to stand by the door.

"I just wanted to congratulate you on the case you won last week. I was out of the country on my boat when I got the news and I wanted to personally tell you before the mass email hit the office."

"Well thank you so much sir. I really enjoyed working this case." Monday told him as professional as possible.

"No thank you for choosing our law firm... I'm telling you now, you have something special, I should've known when I looked at your LSAT score." Mr. Hawk continued while Monday tried to act interested.

"Well anyway... I got a meeting starting in five minutes and I just wanted to let you know that." He looked down at the Apple Watch on his wrist.

"And like I said, you can always move to Chicago and marry me when you graduate Law School." Mr. Hawk told her as they headed out of his office together.

Without responding or acknowledging him at all, Monday headed to her desk where she dived deep into her work. Completing everything ahead of schedule, with the help of Jhene Aiko soothing voice coming out of her air pods, it was time for lunch before she knew it. Snatching up her Gucci bag, Monday practically ran out the office and to Chipotle on the corner. Her empty stomach had been growling the entire morning and a steak bowl had been heavy on her mind. Catching the elevator just in time, she called Shaquita the moment she stepped into the hot sun.

"Hey baby. How you feeling?" Monday asked as the wind blew her jet-black curly hair.

"I'm better now. I been on the phone with Weezy all morning. At first I thought he was gon' be mad that I canceled on him the other day but he was really understanding. Even offered to bring me some Pepto Bismol but I told him I was cool."

"Girl.... Pepto Bismol? That ain't no stomach flu sweetheart... YOU PREGNANT!" Monday giggle into the phone before entering the restaurant.

Shaquita cursed into the phone while Monday placed her steak bowl order. The day she came across the snapchat of Law at the hospital, she lost it, even calling Weezy, ready to risk it all. Monday tried talking to her, but she wasn't having it and had it not been for the "stomach flu" she caught, she would have gone through with it.

"Imma just keep him blocked and until then, you can find me riding Weezy's dick." Shaquita shouted loudly into the phone, causing Monday to laugh.

"Speaking of the devil, this him calling me now. I'll see you when you get home."

After thanking the employee and grabbing her food, Monday headed to the door just as it began to get crowed. Slipping past a few people successfully, she came crashing shoulder to shoulder with a woman with long braids, down to her ass.

"Oh, I am so sorry." Monday turned to the woman and apologized with a smile.

Expecting the same reaction, Monday's smile turned upside down when the lady mugged her. Matching her energy, Monday sized her up before slowly walking away.

"Yeah that's that bitch. I should slap that hoe." Monday heard the woman say before her friend pulled her away.

❧ 18 ☙

B lock walked through the four-bedroom home and shook his head up and down in approval. It was the exact house he used to draw and put on the refrigerator when he was a kid. A two-story red stone brick home equipped with a finished basement and wet bar. A huge backyard with a trampoline and pool for AJ. The new place was tucked off away from the hood but not too far.

"So, Mr. Williams, what do you think? This a pretty nice home for a family man like yourself." Katrina, the realtor, flirted with him, like she had been doing the entire showing.

"I'll take it. Let me know the final amount and I'll cut you a check. Thanks so much and I look forward to hearing from you." Block flashed a smile and replied as the two headed out onto the front porch.

Stepping around the manicured grass and onto the hot pavement, Block hit the alarm on his Jeep and jumped in. Placing his phone on the charger, he dialed Monday's number, letting her know that he was on his way. Stopping at the gas station not far from Shaquita's spot, Block grabbed two bottles of water and a pack of gum before speeding off. Pulling in front of the duplex seven minutes later, he text Monday, letting her know he was out front. With his head bouncing up and down to the sounds of Rod Wave, Block's eyes zoomed in on Monday the moment she stepped foot on the porch. Dressed in a yellow maxi sundress that flowed past her feet, she was undoubtably one of the prettiest women Block ever laid eyes on. Outside of her looks, Monday's personality spoke volumes. Coming across as the stuck-up type at first, Block was surprised to learn that she was the total opposite and actually pretty openminded.

"Hey baby!" She got inside the truck and sang, placing a kiss on his lips as he leaned in for one.

"What's up baby. You hungry?" He asked while she pulled down the sun visor, checking her reflection.

"I am. What you got a taste for?" Monday shifted her body in the seat, facing him and asked.

Biting down on his bottom lip, Block glanced away from the road and at her, his eyes slowly traveling down to his favorite spot in between her legs. Giggling like a silly shy schoolgirl, Monday playfully punched him in the arm.

"I'm serious." She told him before looking down at her ringing phone.

"Shiddd me too but I got you, we finna grab us some chicken and go chill at the Lake Front." Block told her as he headed to Uncle Remus on Madison and Central.

It had been years since he grabbed a bottle, some food, and kicked it with a chick at the Lake Front. When him and Tisha were fresh and in love, they'd hit up the spot at least twice a month, just to talk and clear their mind. Chilling by the water was peaceful and calm, something he needed in the crazy world we lived in.

"Ugghhhh...... this place looks dirty?" Block heard Monday complain the second they pulled up in front of the restaurant.

"The dirty ones have the best food. Come on." He told her before getting out of the car.

Block waited for Monday on the curb, grabbing her hand and dodging traffic as they crossed the busy intersection. Being in her presence made him feel different, yet different in a good way. Since the day they linked, Block hadn't been able to get her off his mind. Arguing everyday with Tisha because he hadn't been home in days was starting to affect him, which was one of the reasons he was moving out and leaving her at the old crib. In Block's mind, they'd share joint custody, he'd continue to pay all her bills, and everything would be straight.

"How can I help you?" Block heard the lady behind the thick glass ask, snapping him out of his trance.

"Aye let me get a ummmmmm....... G-Pan....fried hard with extra mild sauce...."

"Mild sauce? I want ketchup." Monday cut in and said, causing everyone to stare at her.

"Ketchup? Man..... don't nobody eat that shit." Block twisted his head and replied before ordering their drinks.

After waiting thirty minutes for their food and promising her that mild sauce would be the best thing she ever tasted, the two was headed to his ride with greasy bags in hands. Taking the streets until he hit Lake Shore Drive, Block decided to take the long way, simply because he enjoyed vibing and listening to music with her. Lucking up on a spot a few feet from the water, he cut off the air, rolled down the windows, and grabbed their food.

"We about to eat right here?" Monday asked as she took the food he handed to her.

"Yup."

"But Imma make a mess. My dress yellow and...."

"Chill, baby. Relax. Enjoy yo food and try not to eat like you're two." He replied with a smile before handing her extra napkins.

The two sat in the car and smacked away, neither of them uttering a word to one another as they enjoyed their food. Placing all pride to the side, Monday admitted that mild sauce was the best thing since slice bread and vowed to take a jug back with her when she left. The conversation shifted with the mention of her going back to California and Block knew she felt it too.

"Let's go sit on the rocks." Block said, hoping that a change of scenery would change the dynamic of the mood.

Jumping out before she did, Block made it to her side just in time to open the door for her and help her out. The feel from her soft hands had him thinking with his dick, just that fast. Their sexual chemistry was explosive, something neither of them had experienced before. Hand by hand, the two walked along the pathway until they arrived at the rocks.

"It's so beautiful out here." Monday cooed, taking a seat next to him as they both gazed at the starlit skies.

"Yeah. I be trying to tell muthafuckers, Chicago's beautiful beyond all the shit the news show." Block pulled her in close and replied as she rested her head on his shoulder.

"Yeah, it is. I can come out here and look at the sky every night, just to reflect on the type of day I've had at court." Monday closed her eyes and imagined as the cool breeze bless them.

"I can put you in a condo right there.... In those high-rises over there. You'll have the perfect view from your bedroom." Block promised, pointing at a street full of high-rise buildings.

"Only if life was that simple." Monday replied, letting out a long sigh.

"Life is as simple as you make it and everything, I just said.... I STAND TEN TOES ON THAT SHIT!" Block barked, causing Monday to sit up straight and look at him.

The two stared in each other's eyes for a few seconds, without uttering a word. It was like they were trying to see if they could read what was on the other's mind. Block was sure about where he stood in the situation and if he could have things his way, Monday would be in Chicago indefinitely, but he knew it wasn't his call. He was falling in love with her and didn't wanna imagine going back to life after summer without her.

"Block, I think I'm falling in ...."

The sound of his phone ringing cut her short. He had already ignored about seven calls in the past two minutes but the last one was the final straw for her.

"My bad baby, what was you saying?" He asked, putting the phone on vibrate but not quick enough before another call came ringing in.

"Just answer the bitch call.... DAMN!" Monday snapped, scooting over a few inches, giving him space to talk in private.

Letting out a frustrated sigh, Block ignored Tisha's call yet again and made up his mind, for once and for all. He was leaving her and making Monday his, even if that meant convincing her to move from California to Chicago.

❈ 19 ❈

Law did the dash on 290 heading to Shaquita's place. It had been three days since the last time she answered a phone call or text from him. Completely clueless as to why she went MIA all of a sudden, Law prayed it wasn't what he thought it was. Merging into the far-right lane to make his exit at Independence, Law double check the mirrors before making the dash. Safely crossing and emerging from the ramp, he turned up his music and drove the rest of the way, thinking the worst. Last time him and Shaq had a conversation was the morning she cooked them breakfast. He remembered her saying she was swinging by her grandparents' house, fast forward a few hours later, he was blocked on everything. Unfortunately, he was too familiar with the routine, that's why he was pulling up like a mad man, yet again. Parking in front of her place, he killed the engine and jumped out. Going inside his pocket for his key, Law pulled it out and placed it in the locks but it didn't turn.

"This muthafuckn' girl changed the locks!" He barked, punching the front door with a closed fist.

"MAN, YO CAR OUT HERE! OPEN THE DOOR!" Law yelled and banged, drawing eyes from a few passerby's.

"SHAQUITA! OPEN THE DOOR!"

Getting the same response as before, nothing, he went back inside his pocket but pulled out his phone this time. Knowing it was a shot in the dark, he dialed her number with hopes to get through. Getting pissed like he didn't know the outcome already, Law reached out to Block next.

"Aye nigga, Monday with you?" Law called on him and asked, heading back to his car feeling defeated.

"Nah... she at work. What's wrong?" Block questioned from the other end of the line.

"Same goofass shit with Shaq, man. She still ain't answering the phone and won't even let a nigga know what he did wrong this time." Law admitted truthfully, however, those same words caused Block to laugh.

"You know exactly what the fuck you did and what's going on. I told you it was a matter of time before she found out shorty was pregnant and then when the bitch popped up at the hospital, I knew it was over with from there." Block let him have it straight.

Knowing his homie was right, Law ended the call with him and cranked up the engine; he needed to get to the bottom of things before it went any further. Flying down the Dan Ryan, Block knew better than to fuck with a bitch off 63rd the second he ran across Rachel, but his dick did the talking for him. This time, he needed to first see if she reached out to Shaquita and if so, how much did she tell her. Finally feeling like he was too old for the bullshit he was doing, Law asked God to get him out of that situation, with promises never to mess up again. Jumping out on a mission for the second time in an hour, Law stormed up the stairs to Rachel's townhouse and banged on the door. Unlike with Shaquita, Rachel was pulling the door back with a huge smile on her face. Barely able to stomach the sight of her, Law pushed passed and entered.

"You been in contact with my girl?" He stood in the middle of the smoke-filled living room and asked her.

"Define contact?" She laughed but little did she know, she was already skating on thin ice.

"Why you so worried about that bitch when I'm the one carrying your child?" Rachel continued as she strutted towards him in a pair of black boy shorts and Nike sports bra.

"And that's to be determined." Law shot her a look and replied out the corner of his eye.

Rachel was a chick he kicked it with for a few months off and on whenever him and Shaquita was on bad terms. They went through a stretch a few months back when they couldn't seem to get it right and that's when Law made the biggest mistake ever. He remembered the night the condom broke but thought the Plan B pill he made her take the next morning solved the problem.

"How much man?" He leaned against the gray walls and asked pulling out a wad of hundreds in cash.

"How much? What the fuck you mean, how much? How much for what?" Rachel snapped, placing her hands on her hips.

"I want a test at the hospital and if the baby is mine, I'll take care of it, but you and the baby gotta move across the country. I'll give you ten stacks a month to chill out and don't reach out. When shorty turns about five, we can do a custody thing but I know yo type, it's more about pissing my girl off right now than it is about the baby."

"So, let me get this right, that bitch Shaquita can live the life and reap the benefits of being yo wife when ME... the mother of your child has to play side bitch and....."

"SIDE BITCH! THAT'S EXACTLY WHAT YOU ARE.... SO YES..... PLAY YO ROLE.... OR BE A SINGLE MOTHER." Law laid it down for her in black and white.

He was tired of playing nice with bitches like Rachel. Yes, he took fault and full responsibility for getting her pregnant, but he refused to let another human being control his life. He accepted the fact that she wasn't getting an abortion and came to terms with having a child, but he would never let a bitch get the upper hand. Standing straight up, Law headed to the door when Rachel started crying, He didn't have an empathy bone in his body for her and if you asked him, she was getting off easy. Law wasn't dumb, he knew Rachel was keeping the baby solely based off his name in the streets. The Jack Boyz were on every bitch to-do list and getting pregnant by one was like hitting the lottery. In fact, Block was the only one out the crew with kids.

"So, you gon' just offer me money and leave?" Rachel questioned through tears before jumping in front of him, blocking his path.

"Man, girl move!" Law urged, trying his best to get around her.

"You know what. See! I was playing nice, dropping hints and shit for the bitch, but now Imma call her and just tell her.... Flat out..... BITCH YOU ABOUT TO BE A STEP MOMMY!" Rachel screamed before giving off a sinister laugh and dashing to her phone.

"Yup! I'll call Shaquita myself and tell her, it ain't like I ain't got her number." Rachel threatened, going to her contact list and placing the call on speaker.

"HELLLLOOOOO!" Shaquita's voice rang out, causing Law to lose it.

Reaching inside his waist, Law pulled out his pistol and twisted on the silencer, all before Rachel could even notice. With her preparing to tell his girl the worst, wrong or not, he wasn't willing to lose his bitch, so he offed her...... her and "his baby."

🦋 20 🦋

Shaquita woke up the next morning with a slight headache and the sound of an episode of *Martin* playing on B.E.T in the background. She slept like crap the night before and for some reason, she couldn't stop tossing and turning. She had been having bad nightmares for the past few nights as well and she had no idea what contributed to those either. At first she thought it was her new friend Rachel and her post but after blocking Law and talking to Weezy, she thought she was in a better space. The two hadn't officially kicked it, however, their time was coming soon. Coming down with the stomach flu, Shaquita could barely move and the bathroom toilet had become her best friend.

"I'm gone with Block!" Shaquita heard Monday yell out from behind her door before hearing the alarm system set.

Searching for her phone under the pillow, Shaquita finally found it along with a piece of candy she dropped last night. Tossing the sour patch in her mouth, she ignored the nine private calls from either Law or one of his hoes and headed to Facebook. As soon as the app opened, there it was, a friend request from a Rachel BadBitchesOnly Conner. Absent from social media for a few days, Shaq was unsure of how long the request was waiting. Accepting it without thinking twice, she got the shock of her life when she went on her page. Rest in peace statuses from family and friends made her mouth drop to the floor. According to her timeline, Rachel was found dead in an alley a few blocks away from her home. Shocked was an understatement and although she didn't know the woman personally, she still felt some type of way. Scrolling for another hour or so on all social media outlets, Shaquita finally pulled herself out the bed and into the bathroom where she took a shower. Washing her hair and shaving her underarms and legs, Shaq was starting to feel like a new woman, even having an appetite for the first time in days. Throwing on a pair of biker shorts and tank top, Shaquita slid on her gray fluffy Uggs sandals and made her way down the stairs. Hitting the landing, the doorbell rang and for some reason, she knew exactly who it was. Changing the locks on Law wasn't enough to keep him away and although she ignored him, she knew she couldn't do so forever.

"STOP RINGING MY FUCKN' DOORBELL!" She yanked the door open and snapped while Law stood on her doorstep with a smile.

"I'm just happy to see your face. Can I come in and talk?" Law locked eyes with her and asked in a charming voice.

"Nah, you can plead yo whack ass case from right here." She crossed her arms across her chest and told him.

"Okay. Okay. I just wanna know why you change the locks? Why haven't you been answering the phone?"

"Simple. Yo lil deceased ass girlfriend felt the need to show me that she was at the hospital with you the day you got shot. You know that I ---"

"What deceased ass girlfriend?" Law cut her off and asked, causing her to shake her head from side to side.

Shaquita was no fool and although she couldn't prove it, she was sure Law, or The Jack Boyz, had something to do with that girl's murder. Call it a coincidence if you want to, Shaq knew Rachel wanted to tell her something, but unfortunately for her, a bullet got to her first.

"Rachel, a bitch from the hood, a rat... she came up there to check on me.....Hell, a gang of bitches showed their concern but you tripping on her." Law pleaded while Shaquita rolled her eyes to the back of her head.

Smacking her lips and shifting her weight to one side, Shaq half listened while he ran the same game. He loved her and only wanted to be with her. There was nobody else out there for him and nothing will ever come between them again and blah blah blah. Although there was no doubt in Shaq's mind that his feelings were real, it was unfortunate that he didn't know how to love her correctly.

"Law, I love you too but ....."

Quickly turning her heels, Shaq ran at top speed up the stairs and to the bathroom where she emptied last night's dinner in the toilet bowl. She had gone a smooth twenty-four-hours without throwing up and thought she was in the clear until now. Making a mental note to make a doctor's appointment later that day, Shaq stood to her feet and headed to the sink. Brushing her teeth and gurgling with the Scope mouthwash nearby, she took one final look in the mirror before exiting. Entering her bedroom, Shaq froze in her tracks when she noticed Law sitting on her bed with her phone in his hands. She can tell by the look on his face that whatever he came across wasn't something good.

"Why you got my phone in yo hand?" She shuddered, stopping in the bathroom doorway.

"Who is Weezy, Shaquita?" Law slowly stood to his feet and questioned in a calm yet scary tone.

"Why you going through my st – my stuff?" She stuttered, taking a few steps back, however, she collided with the wall.

"I was unblocking myself when a nigga slid through yo line asking was y'all still getting up whenever you felt better?" Law continued with a slow stride towards her.

Shaquita's eyes searched the room for something she could use to defend herself. Her and Law had been together long enough for her to know when he was pissed but this wasn't his normal pissed, he was furious. Honestly, she was afraid for her life and had heard too many stories about the mad boyfriend who murdered his girl in a rage. On top of that, she'd witnessed him take life and not ever think twice about what he did. Law was the type of man, like many, who can dish it out but can't take it. Here he was, ready to catch a body, when he'd done more dirt than the law allows. Spotting her eyes on the dresser, Shaq thought about making a run for it and mace him if need be, but she wasn't about to allow him to hurt her. Never in the years they'd been together had Law put his hands on her but then again, she never got caught cheating. Yeah, technically she hadn't because they never did anything, but niggas never seen it that way.

"Who is Weezy, Shaq and how you know this nigga?" Law now stood in front of her and questioned, making her dash for her keys impossible now.

Trying her best not to stutter because you always seemed guilty whether you were telling the truth or not. Shaquita also searched for the right words to say, careful not to trigger him but feisty enough to let him know she ain't no weak bitch.

"He some nigga that tried talking to me on my way home. I took his number, ain't give him mine. You pissed me off so I called him to have a THOT moment but came down with this damn stomach flu. Still pissed at you, I've been texting him....as you can see.... But that's it.... Nothing else." Shaquita stood up straight and looked him in the eyes and explained.

Unable to read the expression on his face, Shaq became a little worried. He didn't look as angry as he did prior but neither did Jeffery Dahmer before he ripped up and ate them little boys. Hesitant to move, Shaquita stood there until he spoke, his next words shocking her.

"Call that nigga and set it up." Law looked her dead in the eyes and ordered before handing her phone and walking off.

"Oh and change yo number.... If you give that Muthafucker out again...... IMMA KILL YOU, SHAQUITA." He warned before disappearing out the door.

❧ 21 ❧

Monday drove down Lake Shore doing about sixty, listening to her new favorite "Ghetto Gospel" by Rod Wave. If wasn't for Block, she'd still be somewhere sleeping on his music instead, she couldn't turn it off. With only one more day left in her internship, Monday was ready to turn up and celebrate with her summer nigga. Before Block, Monday used to feel suffocated when it came to men she dated, especially when they were spending as much time together as they were. Grooving to the music playing, Monday song her heart out, just as a call came through, interrupting the concert.

"Heart been broke so many times eyyyeeeeeeeee.....Hello!" She answered in the middle of her favorite part.

"Girl that nigga got you listening to his music now. You allll the way gone." Shaquita joked, causing Monday to laugh.

"I'm just in a good mood, that's all. Tomorrow my last day and I can't wait to see my bae tonight." Monday replied, cheesing from ear to ear.

"BITCH U SPRUNG! Listen to you! What y'all got planned tonight?" Shaquita questioned her.

"I have no clue. He told me to be ready in a dress and heels by seven." Monday gushed as she merged lanes.

"DRESSSS? HEEELLLLSSS? We talking about the same Aaron "Block" Williams. What type of dick you sucking cousin cuz I ain't never known that nigga to do no romantic shit like that?"

"That's cuz he ain't never met a topflight bitch like me before." Monday joked, causing Shaquita to erupt in laughter.

"You even talking like that nigga. Girl bye!" Shaq replied once her giggling spell was over.

The two talked for a few more minutes before Shaquita asked her to stop at White Castle and bring something to eat home. Being less than a few blocks away from the restaurant, Shaquita hit up CVS first and then slid through the drive thru to place their order. Getting them both a number two with a raspberry lemonade, Monday turned back up her music and cruised the rest of the way home, munching on fries. Pulling behind Shaq's Audi, she killed the engine, grabbed their food and drinks before making her way in doors. Waiting on the couch like a starving dog, Shaquita jumped up and grabbed her food and ran back to her spot on the sofa.

"Damn girl. Slow down." Monday chuckled, popping a squat next to her cousin and digging in her bag.

Enjoying the extra pickles and onions on her cheeseburger, Monday closed her eyes and danced like a fat kid in a candy store. Both her and Shaquita did the snake as they smacked and enjoyed their meal. Finishing up on the cheese sticks they shared, the girls were good and full as they laid across the couch together.

"I need something sweet now." Shaq mumbled before standing to her feet and heading towards the kitchen.

Monday watched her go inside the snack cabinet and pull out a bag of Cheddar Cheese Ruffles and two Twinkies. Shaking her head from side to side, Monday wondered how Shaq went from having the stomach flu one day and then having the munchies the next. Keeping her own thoughts to herself, Monday laid on the couch until she fell asleep. A notification alert on her phone woke her up, just an hour before Block was scheduled to pick her up. Moving Shaquita's heavy ass off of her legs,

Monday left her there before taking off to her bedroom to get dressed. Showering with a quickness, Monday secured the towel around her before starting on her makeup and hair. Achieving perfection in a matter of twenty minutes, she had that amount of time left as well before Block arrived. Dressing in an all-black backless Valentino dress with a pair of black peep-toe Balenciaga heel. Spraying on her favorite Christian Dior perfume, Monday twirled in the sir, just as the doorbell rang.

"Right on time." She smiled, looking down at the gold link watch on her wrist.

Monday heard Shaq headed to the door so she gathered the rest of her things, put them in her purse, and gave herself one final look over. Pleased with her look, especially the way her ass sat up in the dress, Monday knew for a fact she looked like a snack that night.

"Man, fuck what I got planned. We staying in." Monday heard Block say from behind her.

Standing in the doorway with a smile on his face, she couldn't ignore the tingling between her legs. Dressed in a pair of black distressed jeans with a fresh pair of black Timbs underneath, Block finished his looked with an all-black Gucci collar shirt. Impressed with his attire and scent that filled her nostrils from across the room. Licking his lips from his spot in the doorway, Monday grinned from ear to ear and blushed as the two flirted with their eyes.

"Baby, you look so good." Monday finally glided over to him and complimented while he pulled her into a tight hug.

Closing her eyes and ravishing in the moment, Monday inhaled his smelled, wishing she could capture that moment forever. Block made her feel different, he made her feel safe, and although she frowned her nose up at his type in the past, she was loving everything about his hood ass.

"Let me lift this up real quick, get 'bout nine pumps in, and I'm good." He whispered in her ear while his hands roamed freely under her dress.

Needing a quickie badly, Monday pulled away from his embrace, walked over to the bed, slid her panties to the side and bent over. Looking back at Block who admired the view, Monday's pussy became wetter as she watched him bite down on his bottom lip. Slamming the door shut and locking it, Block finally made his way over to. Rubbing her round ass softly, he then pulled down his pants, pulled out his dick, and glided it inside of her walls.

"Fuccckkkkkk." The two moaned out in unison before Block went to work.

The nine pumps he promised turned into way more as they enjoyed each other's bodies. With plans still in motion for the night, the couple made each other cum within a matter of five minutes. Pleased with the results, Monday rushed off to the bathroom to wash up. Finishing up in there, her and Block finally managed to escape the bathroom and were now headed to the car.

"I'm gone cousin." Monday yelled out to Shaquita, who chucked them both the deuces from her spot on the couch.

Opening the front door, Monday and Block prepared to leave when a black Lincoln town car pulled up in front of the house. Assuming it was Law, the two stayed put on the porch when they noticed the driver get out and open the back door. Watching closer, the driver then made his way to the trunk where he pulled out one suitcase.

"CLOSE MY DOOR!" Shaquita yelled out but neither of them paid her no mind.

"Y'ALL LETTING MY AIR OUT!" She continued to fuss; however, Monday's eyes caused her ears to go mute.

Now watching the driver open the backseat doors, Monday almost collapsed to the ground the second Martin stepped out. Knowing her eyes were deceiving her, she blinked four times with hopes that it'd change, but it never did. Monday watched as Martin tipped the guy before grabbing his bags and making his way up the driveway.

"When Shaq start fucking with lames?" Block chuckled as Martin approached the porch with a smile on his face.

"I told y'all to close my damn doo...... OH SHIT!" Shaquita froze in her tracks, realizing now why Monday was stuck.

"Surprise baby!" Martin finally approached the porch and spoke, forcefully pulling her into a hug.

Monday hesitantly wrapped her arms around him, she was still stunned, and honestly didn't know how to proceed. Martin smiled from ear to ear while Shaquita's mouth still lingered on the ground and then there was Block, whose expression she couldn't read.

"How—How—When—I mean wait.... What you doing here? How you know where I was staying?" Monday replied once she was able to gather her words.

"Well sweetheart, I wanted it to be a surprise, so I talked to your parents who gave me your cousin's address. They thought it would be a good idea as well." Martin looked at each of them, his eyes stopping on Block.

"Did I catch you at a bad time? Am I interrupting something?" Martin quizzed, noticing the similarities in their attire.

"Nah big fella, you ain't interrupting shit. Enjoy your girl. I'll holler at you later, Shaq." Block imparted before walking down the stairs and driving away.

$$\text{❧} \quad 2\,2 \quad \text{❧}$$

In all his twenty-five years on this Earth, Block never felt the way he was feeling the moment he pulled away from Shaquita's house. Hurt wouldn't be the word he used; however, he was most definitely feeling some type of way. The thing was, he knew about her lame ass dude from the beginning but at the time, he didn't care. He had Tisha around, Monday was something fun to do for the summer, therefore, getting his feelings hurt never crossed his mind. Making sure to be a player about the situation, he walked away when in reality, he wanted to lay both they asses out. He could tell from her demeanor that his visit was indeed unexpected but that still didn't take away from how it felt.

Flying down 290 headed back to the hood, Block didn't even bother to cancel the reservations he had, instead, he stopped at the liquor store and grabbed him a bottle of D'usse. Pulling on the block with the guys, he rolled up and poured a cup before chilling on the hood of his car. Just like any other summertime night in Chicago, the streets were filled to capacity with people of all ages. Cars double parked on the street, holding back up traffic for miles. Loud music played out of windows while bitches shook their asses to the beat. It was like a movie or music video the way things played out. With all the commotion and everything going on, he couldn't help but think about Monday. In fact, she hadn't left his mind since he pulled off. Parts of him wanted to go back and wreck shit while other part told him to chill and take that "L".

"Nigga, you good? Shaq just told me what happened. I thought yo ass was gon' be on suicide watch." Law walked up and joked, causing Block's eyes to dart in his direction.

"Yo ass a clown nigga." Block chuckled, handing him the blunt while the two reflected on his night.

"On foe nem.... I would have aired that bitch out. And you just let homie walk in the crib with yo bitch –"

"That ain't my bitch." Block stopped and corrected him before he continued.

"MANNNNNN.... FUCK ALL DAT! You got real ass feelings for shorty and you salty but you handled dat shit like a G." Law told him while pouring himself a cup of the brown liquor.

"But if it helps any, when I was on the phone with Shaq, Monday came in the room crying and shit. Shaquita say she ain't want you to leave and...."

"You got some mo za?" Block cut him off and asked before Law went inside his pocket and pulled out the weed.

"Roll that up cuz I ain't trying to talk about dat shit." He finished saying while filling up his third cup.

Block and his crew kicked it until about two, which was around the time the rain started. Forced to end his night early, he drove home drunk, barely making it safely inside. Struggling with the keys at the door, Block dropped them twice before finally pulling it together. Entering the dark house, he stumbled over a few of AJ's toys before landing on the couch. With the room spinning, he knew he overdid it but at least his mind was Monday free. Closing his eyes and inhaling deeply, Block carefully got up and headed up the stairs. Stopping off in AJ's bedroom first, he removed the phone from his son's hands before tucking him in tighter and kissing him on the forehead. Regardless of whatever Block went through, his son seemed to always brighten up the moment. Leaving his bedroom door slightly cracked, Block crept down the hallway and into his bedroom. Glancing at

Tisha who stirred in her sleep, he went directly inside the conjoined bathroom where he relived himself. Washing his hands and running a towel over his face, Block cut the light out and headed back downstairs.

"So, you barely home and when you here, you sleep on the couch?" Block heard Tisha's loud voice echo through his ears when his foot hit the landing.

Turning around and staring up at her, Block debated whether or not he should respond. The liquor and weed had him feeling good, the last thing he wanted was for his baby mother to blow his night. Making the decision to remain silent, he turned back around and headed towards the linen closet. Pulling the door open, Block grabbed a blanket and pillow before making his way towards his man cave. Thinking maybe Tisha got the picture and went back to bed, he tossed the things on the couch to grab a bottle of water out the fridge.

"Aaron, if you gon' ignore me in my house.... YOU CAN GET THE FUCK OUT!" She came yelling down the stairs screaming with her phone in hand.

"In due time shorty. In due time." He calmly turned to her and replied before stepping around and walking away.

"And I know who yo lil bitch is too. Un huhhhh.... Thought I was dumb, didn't you? I know she works downtown and likes to eat Chipotle for lunch or whatever." Tisha taunted, smacking her lips with every other word she spoke.

Knowing which buttons to push and when to push them, Block allowed Tisha to run her mouth. Little did she know, his plan was already in motion and he was set to pick up the keys to his new crib in a few days. Block hadn't spoken a word to Tisha about it but figured now was the perfect time.

"Me and my son will be moving out in 'bout a week or so. Imma pay all the bills here, yo car paid off, and I'll still slide you something every month. As far as Lil Aaron, we can do a weekly thing since school is about to start. Don't worry about no expenses concerning him, I got him." Block looked her dead in the eyes and explained before turning and walking away.

Knowing her like the back of his hand, he knew it was only a matter of time before she got to flipping out and acting crazy. Tisha was dramatic and when hurt, she was a dangerous woman.

"So, you think you finna leave me and start a family with Sunday? Well nigga you got another thing coming." She warned while he took a seat on the black leather sectional in their living room.

Block watched Tisha unlock her phone and place a call. Chuckling aloud because he knew for a fact, she had no one to call. Neither her daddy, her brother, or her toughest uncle could fuck with Block and she knew that too. Placing the call on speaker, Block's eyes bucked at the response from the person on the other end.

"9-1-1, what's your emergency?"

"My baby daddy just beat me up. His name is Aaron Williams, we live at ....."

Block blacked out while Tisha reported a false domestic violence call. He couldn't believe she was stooping that low, calling the cops was a game that they never played. Slowly standing to his feet, Block let out a deep sigh before grabbing his phone and keys. Placing them both in his pocket, he made his way over to her just before she ended the call.

"I'll beat that bitch ass and never allow you to see AJ again before I let you leave me." Tisha threatened through tears, but it was too late.

Block had his hands wrapped around her neck, struggling to breathe, fighting for air, he lifted her off the ground. At that moment, catching a domestic was worth it and since 12 was already on the way, he choked the bitch out.

🎗 23 🎗

Shaquita pulled in front of Southern Soul Food restaurant and killed the engine. Taking a deep breath, she took a look inside first before getting out of the car. From outside, she could see a few people waiting, but it wasn't too crowded, so she entered. Pleased with the décor and aroma coming from the kitchen, Shaq took her spot in line and waited patiently. Humming to the sounds of Tina Turner that played in the bathroom, Shaquita made a mental note to watch "What's Love Got To Do With It" when she made it back home. Stepping up a few feet, it was finally her turn to order.

"Hey hunny, how can I help you?" An older black woman with moles on her face asked with a warm smile.

"I'll take the catfish dinner, fried hard with greens and baked macaroni and cheese for my sides, please." Shaq replied with a grin, matching her energy.

After ordering her something to drink, Shaquita thanked the woman before paying and taking her ticket. Noticing a photo gallery on the wall when she walked in, she made her way towards it to get a closer look. Pictures of customers, celebrities, and events that took place there hung on a wall near the restroom. Shaquita's eyes scanned every photo closely, hoping she came across what she was looking for.

"NUMBER 28!" Shaq heard the woman yell out, pulling her away too soon.

"Thank you so much ma'am. Can I have a few more napkins please?" She requested.

"Sure sweetheart, anything else I can get ya?"

"Well actually there is. I'm a journalist in my last year in school and I'm doing a piece on black owned businesses in the neighborhood and wanted to feature Southern Soul Food in my story. Nothing major, it's basically me interviewing the owner, asking him some questions, getting to know him better." Shaquita lied with a straight face.

"Oh, okay sure. I'll be sure to tell Billy about it. You got a card or number or something I can give to him?"

"Ummmm.... I just handed out my last business card. How about I leave my name and number and he can give me a call."

"Sure, no problem sweetie, I'll be sure to pass that along." The cashier told her before tying up the plastic bag and handing to her.

"Thank you so much. Enjoy your day!"

Shaquita skipped out of the restaurant with a huge smile plastered across her face. It was easier than she thought, getting closer to the man who was supposedly her father. With giving up the task of talking to her mother about it, Shaq decided she'd investigate herself since so many people around her seemed to be lying. Taking the streets home, Shaquita thought about life and the possibility of this man Billy being her dad. Connecting her dying phone to the charger, Shaq shuffled through the playlist trying to find something good to listen to. Settling on the sounds of Cardi B, she danced to beat until her a call came through, interrupting.

"Hello." She answered on the second ring, turning the volume up to hear better.

"What's up beautiful! Am I seeing you tonight?" Weezy asked, his deep voice filling her car speakers.

"You sure are baby. I booked the room and I'll be there by nine." Shaquita assured him before ending the call and turning the music up.

Singing and dancing the rest of the ride home, Shaq enjoyed the time alone, it allowed her to reflect on life. With her vacation coming to the end, she needed to clear her mind before going back to that place. Pulling in behind Block's car in the driveway, she grabbed her food and made it inside before the rain started. Going directly to the kitchen, Shaquita called out to Monday who came joining her a few seconds later.

"You wanna try this food I got from this soul food place?" Shaq asked before taking a fork full of macaroni and cheese in her mouth.

"You got something with some mild sauce on it? I'll take that." She quizzed while her eyes surveilled her plate.

"You and this mild sauce." Shaq giggled as she poured Louisiana Hot Sauce on her fried catfish.

"Speaking of.... You talked to Block yet?"

"Nope." Monday quickly turned on her heels and replied, heading back towards the bedroom.

"You reach out?" Shaq questioned.

"Nope."

"Well did that nigga reach out?"

"Nope! Fuck Block, I leave in a couple of days anyway." Monday hissed before disappearing behind the bedroom doors.

Shaquita laughed to herself, all the while filling her belly with scrumptious meal that sat in front of her. She didn't pay Monday much mind especially since she knew she was stunting. Monday fell for Block, hard, whether she wants to admit it or not and vice versa. The night Martin popped up, Shaq's mouth fell to the floor. No one had a clue he was flying out and that was evident from Monday's reaction. She cried to Shaquita the entire two days Martin was in Chicago.

After demolishing her food, Shaquita headed upstairs to take a nap before her date. With her mind racing, she was barely able to nod off and when she did, it was time for her start getting ready. Showering and dressing took a little under an hour for her to get complete. Pleased with her appearance, Shaquita sprayed on her favorite perfume, Chanel No. 5, and took a final look in the mirror. Dressed in all black cat-suit from Fashion Nova, Shaquita's curves looked perfect under the thin material. She knew she looked good and this time it was done effortlessly. Making sure she had everything she needed in her purse, she shot Law a text before heading out the door. Driving to The

Hyatt in Oakbrook, which was about thirty minutes away, Shaquita checked in at the front desk.

"Hello. I have reservations for tonight."

"Great! Can I have your name please?" The friendly front desk receptionist asked after finishing up a previous task.

"Tonya Coleman."

"No problem, I'll just need your ID and the card you used to reserve the room."

After providing the requested information, Shaq was headed to room 202 with the keycard in hand. Checking in under an alias was easier than she thought, she just prayed the rest of the night went the same way. Upon entering the room, Shaquita closed all the blinds before turning on the tv and laying across the bed. Snatching up her phone to check out the time, Shaq's heart began to race when a call came through.

"What's up shorty you good?" Weezy questioned while she tried to pull herself together.

"I'm good. Just waiting on you. I'm in room 202."

"Bet, I'm on my way. Give me 'bout twenty minutes." His deep voice replied before the call ended.

Standing to her feet, Shaquita walked over to the bar inside the room where she poured herself a shot of Hennessey. Not a fan of brown liquor, however, it was exactly what she needed to get through the rest of the night. After taking a second swig to calm her nerves, Shaquita began to feel more relaxed. In the midst of watching reruns of *Family Matters*, there was two light knocks on the door that seemed to still startle her.

"Pull it together Shaquita. Pull it together." She mumbled, trying to give herself a pretalk as she made her way to answer the door.

Standing on her tippy toes to look out the peephole, Shaq took a long deep breathe before pulling the door open. Standing in front of her, just as fine as she remembered, was Weezy. Dressed in all black like an omen, the diamonds around his neck and wrist glistened, adding light to his dark look. With his dreads braided neatly to the back and the crisp lining made Weezy easily one of the most attractive men she ever laid eyes on.

"You gon' give a nigga a hug or nah?" He held his arms open and questioned as Shaquita entered and melted inside.

His cologne attacking her nostrils and the tight grip he had on her ass made her relax a little. Positive that it was the Henny, Shaq was just thankful for the liquor courage that was coming over her. Inviting him inside, Shaquita grabbed his hand and led him to the couch where she turned on the television in there. She knew Weezy didn't come over to watch television or talk, however, she needed to buy a little time.

"What you drinking?" Shaq stood in between his legs and asked while he stared at her like a piece of meat.

"I'll take a cup of that Henny you got over there." He replied, his eyes darting in the direction of the wet bar.

"I got you Daddy. Coming right up." She said with a flirtatious smile before walking away and making the drinks.

Returning back to the couch, Shaquita handed Weezy his cup and took a seat next to him. Knocking back hers first, Weezy followed suit and did the same, except his had a different affect.

"So how was your day baby?" Shaq scooted closer to him and asked, taking her hands and rubbing them over his head.

"Shidd.... Ummmm... Yeah.... My day.... My day was.... My day was...."

And just like that, Weezy was out. Shaquita had no idea the drugs Law had given her to place in his drink would work so fast.

$\maltese$ 24 $\maltese$

With the internship over and summer coming to an end, it was a bittersweet moment for Monday. She got an offer letter from Kirkland and Ellis that practically guaranteed her a position at their law firm when she passed the bar. Knowing more than lately she wouldn't accept the position, she still put it in her back pocket, just in case. Since being done at the law firm and not speaking to Block, Monday lounged around the house until it was time for her leave. The night Martin showed up, Monday didn't know what to do. She had never in her life been in that type of situation before, which was evident by her reaction. Martin asked a few questions and of course, she lied and avoided the conversation as much as possible. After lying about being on her period and having a toothache, Monday was able to avoid sex and head with her man. She wasn't in the mood and if she was being completely honest, he wasn't Block. Monday contemplated day in and day out whether she should reach out to him or not. She missed him so much and the fact he hadn't hit her up wasn't sitting too well with her. She knew exactly what she was getting herself into when she took a bite out of the forbidden fruit, however, she didn't expect to fall in love in the process.

"Monday, you like this?" She heard Shaq say, snapping her out of her love trance.

Looking up and following her voice, Monday's eyes landed on her cousin who held up Gucci's latest collection of fall bags.

"I mean... they aight." She nonchalantly replied before burying her face in her phone.

"UGH girl. Bring yo ass on.... Acting all heartbroken and shit. I told yo ass not to ---"

"Shaqqqqq.... SHUT THE FUCK UP! I ain't trying to hear nun dat right now." Monday snapped, causing Shaquita to stop in her tracks right in the middle of Rosemont mall.

"Girrrllllll.... When you start talking like that?" Shaq asked while clutching her invisible pearls.

Monday couldn't help but laugh at her cousin and although she didn't mean to take her angry out on Shaq, she was working her nerves. Now was not time for her "*I told you so*" speech. She knew that she didn't mean any harm, however, now was not the time. She hated herself for not being able to get Block out of her mind. Any and everything reminded her of him. How could someone you've known for such a small amount of time have such a huge impact on your life?

"Let's head to the food court first. I want some pizza and nuggets from McDonalds." Shaquita craved aloud, causing Monday to glance at her out the corner of her eyes.

Shaking her head from side to side, Monday followed Shaquita as they got in line at McDonalds. Starving but knowing for sure she didn't want anything from the golden arches, Monday stood to the side while Shaq ordered her food. Laughing aloud at her as she added two apple pies and a medium fry to it, Monday pulled out her phone, silently praying she had a message or something from Block. Smacking her lips when she found out that her prayers went unanswered, she stuffed her phone back in her pocket.

"Okay, I'm ready. The pizza joint right over there." Shaq pointed and lead the way while Monday dragged behind.

Pulling her phone back out, Monday read over a new message from Martin when she came colliding with another woman.

"Oh my God! I am so sorry." She looked up and apologized for her clumsiness.

"Watch where the fuck you going next time."

Monday took a few steps back and squinted her eyes. She remembered seeing the woman from somewhere before but couldn't put her finger on it. Knowing it was a mistake on her part, Monday tried ignoring her by remaining quiet and walking around her.

"That's what I thought. I can't believe he want that scary ass bitch." She heard the woman say and that's when it her.

"Ohhhhhh.... You the bum ass baby mother? Hi, I'm Monday.... A real bitch.... Nice to meet you." She said, extending her arm for a handshake.

"I'M ABOUT TO BEAT THIS BITCH ASS!" Tisha roared, handing her friends her purse and phone.

"Tisha, cool it. You ain't gon' buss a grape in a fruit fight." Shaquita appeared out of nowhere and said, stepping in between the two.

"Shaquita, I ain't never had a problem with you but this bitch fucking my nigga and ---"

"And take that L, sis." Monday laughed hysterically from behind Shaq's back.

"I get all that and I'll be salty too but take that up with Block cuz you already know how I get down.... Let's go Monday." Shaq grabbed Mo' by the hand and said to Tisha and her friends.

Sticking her tongue out as Shaquita pulled her away, Monday couldn't believe Ms. Babymomma had the audacity to approach her. She had completely forgotten about the run in at Chipotle and couldn't help but think that things would have played out differently if Shaquita wasn't there. Never claiming to be a fighter, Monday wasn't a hoe either and often had to prove herself. Taking the food to the car, Monday ate half of Shaq's pizza while they drove home, discussing the incident. Her stay in Chicago started off perfect but now that it was time to leave, things were crumbling down.

"I should have stopped at Walgreens to get some sunflower seeds and a snicker." Monday heard Shaq say before they exited the car.

"Shaq, when is the last time you had yo period?" Monday cut her eyes at her cousin and asked.

"Why? It ain't like my shit regular anyway." She placed the key inside the door and replied as the two stepped inside the air-conditioned home.

"Wellllll.... You've been eating a lot and I can't help but notice how fat yo face getting." Monday dropped the bags in the middle of the floor and told her.

"Bitch.... What is you trying to insinuate? I ain't ----"

Shaquita couldn't finish her sentence, she took off running to the closest bathroom, the one inside of Monday's room. Shaking her head from side to side, Mo' followed behind her but instead, she went inside the closet and pulled out a white plastic CVS bag. Pulling out two pregnancy tests that she purchased purposely for this exact moment. She had been teasing Shaquita for a few weeks now about being pregnant, noticing her eating habits and that stomach flu that seemed to come and go. Ignoring anything she had to say, Monday went behind her back and got the test without her knowing.

"It must have been that pizza cuz ---"

"I had the pizza too and I'm good." Monday cut her off and stated before flipping over the test and reading the instructions.

"What's that?" Shaq quizzed, walking over to where Monday stood to get a better look.

"It's a test and ..."

"I ain't taking no test.... FOR WHAT? I ain't pregnant!" Shaquita defensively told her while crossing her arms across her chest.

"Okay and if you ain't pregnant then, what's really the problem? I brought you two, just in case yo ass in denial." Monday chuckled, handing her both tests.

"Ain't no need for two. I know the first gon' be negative but ummmmm.... I ain't the only one who been around here fucking raw. Maybe you need to take one for yourself." Shaquita said, trying to put the same fear in Monday's heart.

"BITCH YOU TRIED IT!" She blurted out loudly in her face and said before snatching the test out of her hands.

Without saying another word, Shaquita headed upstairs with her test while Monday went inside the bathroom with hers. Pissing on the stick, Monday laughed to herself thinking about the reverse psychology Shaquita tried to use on her. Just like there was no doubt in Monday's mind that Shaq was pregnant. There was no doubt in her mind that she wasn't. After washing her hands and placing the pregnancy test on a napkin, she headed upstairs where she found Shaquita finishing up.

"Now all we gotta do is wait." Shaq placed her test next to Monday's and said before the two took a seat on the edge of the tub.

"I know you work at an abortion clinic or what not but.... You gon' keep yo baby, right?" Monday turned to Shaq and asked, just as the timer went off on her phone.

Playfully punching her in the arm, Shaquita stood up first and headed to the sink while Monday stayed put. Although she was anxious for Shaq, she wanted her to be the first to know. Standing at the sink, staring down at both tests, she didn't move nor utter a word, and that's what made Monday nervous. Following suit, she too stood up and headed towards the sink, stopping just behind her but not enough to see over her shoulder.

"Okay so the instructions said, there will be two lines if you pregnant and one if you not. How many you see cousin?" Monday stood on her tippy toes and questioned, becoming more anxious by the second.

"There's --- There's ---- There's FOUR lines cousin. Two on mine and two on yours." Shaquita turned to her and announced, sending Monday's world crashing down.

❧ 25 ❧

"**N**igga, you gon' propose again?" Law heard Block say the minute they pulled inside of Chaz's estate.

"Ain't that's what the fuck I just said? I mean it when I say I'm done with the cheating shit. That Rachel incident scared me Lord, I ain't even gon' cap." Law killed the engine on his Jeep and replied before the two got out the truck.

Law knew he dodged a bullet with the pregnancy situation and in all honesty, he was done for real this time. There wasn't a bitch on Earth bad enough for him to risk his relationship again. Law knew he was going to have to put in work if he wanted to gain her trust back, however, he was fine with that. Shaquita was worth it but it was fucked up it took him almost losing her to find that out.

"Hello Mr. Block and Mr. Law. Mr. Chaz will meet with you in the backyard today." Maria appeared on the porch and smiled before leading them around the back and to the biggest backyard he had ever seen in his life.

No bullshit, it was damn near size of a football field, making Law feel like a groupie the way he lusted over the space. Him and Block always talked about getting a crib and making their spot like Chaz and luckily for them, it was already in the making. After passing the pool, slide and jacuzzi, the guys finally stumbled on Chaz who was sitting alone at a patio table, smoking a cigar and drinking Cognac.

"My boys! What's up?" Chaz stood to his feet and greeted them, pulling them into a manly hug.

Law and Block looked at each other out the corner of their eyes, both thrown off by his gesture. Usually Chaz give them a head nod, nothing more than a fist pump or handshake, yet today, he was touchy feely. Tossing that to the back of their minds, they then took a seat across from him.

"Maria, bring me two more Cubans and drinks for them as well." Chaz instructed and before they could decline, his housekeeper disappeared in the house.

"How are you boys today?" Chaz took a hard pull from his cigar and asked, his eyes shifting back and forth between Law and Block.

"Shid. We straight." Block spoke up first, just as Maria appeared from inside with their cigars and drinks.

"That's what I like to hear." Chaz replied, knocking back his drink while Maria poured him another one.

At first Law couldn't put his finger on it but now it was clear as day, Chaz was drunk as fuck. Never on the talkative side, the guys could tell that he was lit.

"I wanna commend y'all on how y'all handled that Weezy situation. Apparently the lil nigga was in his feelings about the way I ran my business. Y'all was fast and efficient, that's something I look for in teammates." Chaz closed out with, leaving Law and Block feeling like the man.

"Thank you."

"Yeah 'ppreciate it." Block followed behind Law and chimed in and said before taking a sip the cup.

A few seconds of silence allowed the men to reflect on their own thoughts. Thinking about the things he had going on in life made him knock his glass back and immediately pour himself another. Glancing over at Block who did the same, Law knew his homie was dealing with problems of his own. He hadn't been back to his house since the night Tisha called the cops and whether he admit it or not, Monday's boyfriend popping up fucked him up a little. Since they were kids,

Block had been emotionless, however, baby girl from Cali had something over him.

"Y'all sure y'all straight? It looks like y'all had more issues than just Weezy." Chaz filled up yet another glass and said, causing both Law and Block to laugh.

"Yeahhhhh.... See! I know those looks and I'm willing to bet my last million in the bank, it's women problems." Chaz continued as if he was reading both of their minds.

"Aye Chaz, you ever marry?" Law took a pull from the cigar and questioned after realizing he'd never seen him with any women.

"MARRIED? ME? Hell naw. Relationships ain't never seemed to work for me and it's been that way since I lost my first love." He replied, sending the conversation in a direction in which it was not intended to go.

"Oh Shit. Sorry for your loss man." Block looked over at him and empathized.

"Aw nah young buck, she ain't dead... She just left a nigga." Chaz told them, filling the entire backyard with laughter.

"Yeahhhh man... I fucked up with her but that was twenty- three years ago and I'm still not fully over it." Chaz let it be known, giving their young minds something to think about.

"Trust, I know.... I been fucking up so bad but if I lose my girl, Imma spazz." Law spoke his truth, meaning each and every word.

"So, what exactly did you do? How you fuck up?" Law followed up with and asked, wondering how his damages compared to Chaz's.

Taking a deep breath, both Law and Block waited patiently to hear his response. This was the most Chaz had ever opened up and they looked forward to getting some advice from a vet, however, nothing could prepare them for what he said next.

"I fucked my girlfriend's twin sister."

UNTITLED

1995

Chaz pulled in front of the red brick house on the corner of 87th and Bishop and killed the engine to his brand-new black Ford Taurus. Checking his Motorola car phone for the time, Chaz then made sure his pistol was on him before he finally got out the car. Taking a look up and down the street, he made his way over to the wired fence gate and stopped.

"FOR SALE?" He said aloud, reading the words on the red and white sign lounging from the green grass.

"What up Chaz?" Marcus, one of the kids from the neighborhood spoke, as he walked past.

"Aye Marcus, come here. You seen my girl around?" He quizzed while his eyes traveled back to the sign.

"Oh, you ain't heard either huh? Pastor Valentine and First Lady moved this morning. They took the twins and June and left, ain't told nobody nothing. From what I hear, the kids didn't even know they was moving until today." Marcus reported.

"MOVED? WHERE? WHERE THEY TAKE MARSHA?" He screamed, his anger taking over quickly.

"Nobody knows man. They changed their cell numbers and all. Aye, I'm

sorry bro." Marcus said before walking away and leaving Chaz along with his thoughts.

Getting back inside the car, Chaz slammed his fist against the steering wheel and yelled. He knew sooner or later this was going to happen, he just didn't expect it so soon. The up and coming man in the streets but a menace to society if you asked the parents of his girlfriend. Chaz and Marsha secretly dated the last two years of high school. The daughter of a pastor, they didn't accept or approve of the life and path Chaz was headed down. A hustler at 18, he was on his way to the top and Marsha was who he wanted to take with him. Talking to her the night before, Chaz promised her no matter what happened, he'd always be there and that there was nothing her parents could do to stop them from being together. But he was wrong. Cranking up the car, Chaz prepared to pull off when blue and white lights along with sirens pulled behind him. With his gun on his lap and a couple packs on him, Chaz knew where this was headed.

1997

Two years in prison and Chaz was finally a free man at twenty-years old. With that case now behind him, Chaz planned on hitting the streets and making up for lost time. Outside his mother and older sister, he didn't have anyone there for moral support, however, that only made him a better man. With no word from Marsha in those twenty-four months, Chaz was finally able to move on and get her out of his system. Picking up exactly where he left off, it didn't take Chaz long before he was making money moves. Everything was going well and as planned, until he ran into an old friend at a hotel party.

"Oh my Goddddd... Heyyyy Chaz," Marcia's loud voice rang through the halls of The Residence Inn.

Doing a double take, Chaz's heart fell in his stomach when who he thought was Marsha approaching him turned out to be her twin sister. Walking towards him with her arms wide open, Chaz fell into her embrace and just like that, he missed Marsha all over again. Hearing how his first love was away at college living her best life made Chaz feel some type of way. Here he was, missing her and thinking about her the whole first year of his bid and she ain't think about him twice. Chaz and Marcia ended up drinking and vibing the rest of the night. They were having such a good time that; they got their own personal room next door to the party. With Henny in his system, Chaz started to imagine that Marcia was Marsha and that's when it all happened.

Unbeknown to him, not only did he get Marcia pregnant that night, he also *had a two-year old daughter that he knew nothing about. When Pastor Valentine moved them away, it was because they found out that Marsha was pregnant with Shaquita. A pawn in the game, Chaz had no idea that Marcia was sleeping with him to get back at her sister nor did Marcia reveal that he had a child. A petty rivalry amongst twin sisters that went too far and now they were paying for it, twenty-three-years later.*

❧ 26 ❧

Monday struggled to zip up the first suitcase, instantly regretting all the shopping she did while she was there. With Block to blame for the majority of her things, she still had three more bags full of new clothes to take back to California with her. Flopping down on top of it, Monday began to bounce up and down with hopes that'd help. Her frustration growing by the minute, Monday started to fuss, which eventually lead her to crying. As a matter of fact, she hadn't stopped crying since she found out she was pregnant. After going to Walgreens and grabbing four more tests, both her and Shaquita took two more, getting the same result. Heartbroken wasn't the word, there was no word to describe the way she was feeling.

"You still ain't got that suitcase closed?" Shaq walked in and asked before laying across the bed.

"Fuck this suitcase. Fuck all this shit." She replied, wiping the tears from her eyes and joining her cousin on the bed.

"Awww Pooh. Come here." Shaq said to her before pulling Monday close in.

Shaquita was handling the news pretty well, in fact, she was excited about her journey on becoming a mom. She still hadn't told Law yet and Monday thought it was because she was still there. Monday could tell Shaquita was holding back and although being pregnant was the worst for her, she was genuinely happy for Shaq. Her and Law's story was different than hers and Block, therefore, the reactions were completely opposite.

"I can't believe this shit. I came to Chicago for an education and I'm leaving with a baby. That's crazy. What type of luck do I have?" Monday cried into her hands while Shaq rubbed the small of her back.

"Don't look at it that way. You know babies are a blessing and although this wasn't your plan, it was God's plan, cousin." Shaq unintentionally preached.

"God's plan my ass.... God need to stop playing with me. What am I supposed to do? Get an abortion? That ain't happening." Monday sat up and said aloud, talking to both Shaquita and herself.

Monday was pro-choice and she was personally against abortions, well, in situations like hers. She wasn't raped and knew the consequences that came with having unprotected sex all summer. As smart as she was, she was still dumb, Monday was so wrapped up in Block, neither pregnancy nor STDs crossed her mind.

"So, what you gon' do?" Shaquita sat up alongside her and quizzed.

"Go home. Live my truth. I'll be done with my first year of law school by the time I give birth. Sit a semester out and go hard the next. One kid ain't stopping the show." Monday giggled before standing to her feet.

Wiping the last of her tears, Mo' stood in the middle of the floor and let out a deep breath. She needed to hear it aloud for it to register. She wasn't the first pregnant law student; therefore, she knew it could be done. Her parents would be disappointed at first, but they'd get over it. The truth was, she was grown, and it was time she started moving around her parents like an adult. The only other thing that mattered was.....

"What about Martin?" Shaq quizzed as if she was reading her mind.

"We didn't have sex while he was here, so there's no way it could be his and since I was on my period when I arrived in Chicago, means I wasn't pregnant when I left either. He can either accept it or I'll accept being a single mother."

"SINGLE MOTHER? You know Block ain't no dead beat and..."

"And I didn't plan on telling Block." Monday cut her eyes at Shaquita and made known before continuing packing.

"That's selfish as fuck of you and I want you to know that. What harm is it in telling that man that he has a baby? What's gon' happen? Other than you getting all the help you need AND more." Shaq jumped to her feet and retorted as she headed towards the door.

The sound of the doorbell ringing interrupted what was about to get ugly. It was unlikely for the favorite duo to bump heads and the times they did, it never ended well. When Monday said she didn't plan on telling Block, she wasn't thinking about him or his feelings in that moment. She was thinking about the stress that would come with being Block's baby momma, and she didn't want to be anybody's baby momma for that matter. All she wanted to do was have a little fun and enjoy her summer, not become someone's mother.

"Monday come here." Shaq's loud yells from the living room snapped her out of her trance.

Dropping the clothes in hand on the bed, Monday headed to see why she was calling her name so loudly. Upon entering the living room, she stopped in her tracks and stared at Block and Law, who stared at her back. Immediately the wheels in her heads began to turn as she wondered what the look on their faces meant. Did Shaquita snitch and tell them both about the pregnancies or did something else happen? With Monday's eyes eventually drifting off to Block, it was her first time seeing him since Martin's visit and the sight of him made her eyes water. Monday loved that man and it was in that moment she realized it. She'd never got these types of butterflies from Martin nor has he ever made her feel secure the way Block does. Her mind was already cloudy before he got there, and it had only gotten worse.

"Aye. We got sum we need to tell y'all." Law broke the silence and said in a calm yet weary voice.

Both Monday and Shaquita looked at each other before slowly walking over to the couches. Each of their minds racing, wondering what it was they had to say to them. Nothing but bad scenarios played through Monday's head, trying to figure it out. Was someone dead? Was someone about to die? Was someone dying? Questions after questions skated through her mind as she took a seat next to Shaq but across from Block.

"What's wrong? What happened? Y'all scaring us." Shaq said, speaking up for them both.

"We got somebody y'all BOTH should meet." Block looked Monday in the eyes and replied while Law walked over to the front door.

"Meet who?" Monday finally found the words to ask but neither of them answered her, instead in walked a tall slender man with a salt and pepper beard.

"Who the fuck is this y'all letting in my house?" Shaq sprung to her feet and snapped while Monday stared into his familiar eyes.

"She acts just like Marsha." The unknown man spoke from his spot at the door.

"And how he knows my Auntie?" Monday rose to her feet and questioned behind her cousin.

"Damn... Y'all look like twins. WOW!" The stranger wailed as he walked further into Shaquita's house.

"WHO ARE YOU?" Shaq yelled out, her eyes daring his.

"I'm who you came looking for. Y'all's father.... Billy Chaz."

$\overset{\text{❀}}{}\ \ 27\ \ \overset{\text{❀}}{}$

"So, what did he say when you gave him his car keys back?" Shaquita asked Monday as she drove the expressway to O'Hare Airport.

"Nothing. He told me to take care and the nigga hit me with a forehead kiss." Monday replied, lowering her chin into her chest.

Seeing her hurt broke Shaq's heart into pieces. On top of them finding out they were pregnant, they both learned the truth behind all the lies they were told. When Chaz ran the story from top to bottom, the girls couldn't believe their ears. After calling both of their mothers and getting them to confirm the story, both Shaquita and Monday were lost. Their mothers never had the typical sister-sister relationship and neither of them knew why. Figuring it was weird especially for identical twins to be so distant, they still wouldn't have thought in their wildest dreams it was because of a man. Monday's mom was keeping her away from Chicago for more reasons than one. And apparently it was a sworn secret amongst their family that was never supposed to get leaked. Confused at who they should be mad at most, Shaquita and Monday decided to protect their peace for the babies they were carrying and deal with the madness later.

"And you still not gon' tell him about the baby?" Shaq glanced over at her and asked, breaking the brief silence in the car.

"Nope. I --- "

"You know you doing exactly what our mothers did right? You bringing a child into this world and --- "

"I know what I'm doing Shaq and although it's not what YOU would do, I'm doing what's best for me. Block got a whole lot going on already here with the crazy ass baby momma he got now."

"Well Block moved out. Got him a nice house in Glen View. Yeah.... Law told me." Shaq cut her eyes at Monday and replied before focusing back on the road.

"You know what, Shaquita? I liked you way better when we were cousins cuz bitch you are a horrible sister." Monday twisted around in the passenger seat and told her before the two shared a laughed.

The sister part came easy for them, it was the lies from the old heads that tried to rip them apart. They had a story to tell their grandchildren and vowed as sisters to never be like their mothers. Pulling up to American Airlines terminal, Shaq's heart began to sink the closer she got. Spending the past three months with her sister-cousin was everything she could have imagined. Out of her element, Monday was still able to let her hair down and adjust, although the outcome wasn't the ideal one. Hitting the locks to the doors and trunk, Shaquita turned to Monday who had tears in her eyes.

"Awwwww.... We gon' be crying the whole nine months?" Shaq wiped her own tears and said before getting out the car.

Embracing in a huge hug, the girls cried together, on each other's shoulders for a few seconds before releasing their grip. They had been through so much over the last weeks and although they didn't think it was possible, they were closer now than they ever were before.

"Let me go before I miss my flight." Monday said as they pulled the two suitcases out and placed them on the curb.

"Well call me as soon as you land. I love you." Shaquita replied, pulling her into another hug.

"I love you too. See you later." Monday turned around and walked away towards curbside check-in.

Jumping back inside her car, Shaquita headed home where she

planned on showering, eating, and getting in bed. Making a stop at Wendy's drive-thru, Shaq ordered her food before officially taking it in. Pulling inside her driveway, she smiled when she noticed Law's car parked on the side. When she told him the news about the baby the night before, he flipped out. Shaquita swear she seen a tear, although he denied it. Getting out the car, Shaq hit the locks before making her way up the stairs and to the door. Stepping one foot inside, she stopped and looked down at the red and white rose petals that led throughout the path. The sound of soft music and burnt chicken came from the kitchen. Making her way through the dimly lit house, Shaquita stopped and laughed as she watched Law attempt to cook baked chicken.

"I ain't know I was supposed to put some type of liquid at the bottom of the pan." He turned to her and said as he pulled out the blackened chicken pieces.

"It's okay baby. I got you a 4 for 4 but it's the thought that counts." Shaquita smiled, placing the food on the counter before joining him near the stove.

Melting into his arms, Shaq closed her eyes and let out a deep breath. She loved Law despite their path and knew by the way he handled her that he loved her too. But she meant what she said, one more fuck up and she was done with his ass. Opening her eyes when she felt Law pulling away, Shaquita's eyes followed him as he knelt down on one knee.

"Law don't st---"

"Shhhh.... Be quiet." He cut her off, causing her to giggle, however, she remained silent.

Going inside his pocket, Law pulled out a maroon velvet ring box. Opening it up, Shaquita's eyes bucked at the sight of the custom loose diamond ring dripped in white gold. It was stunning, in fact, one of the most beautiful rings she had ever laid her eyes on.

"This is not an engagement ring and I'm not proposing, however, I am promising. I'm promising to be the man you want, need, and dreamed of. I promise to be the best father to our children. I promise to never hurt you again and I promise to stand on this shit ten toes. I love you Shaquita and although I'm not proposing now, you will definitely be my wife." Law glanced up in her eyes and promised as tears streamed down her face.

Extending her left arm, Shaquita allowed him to place the radiant ring on her finger while she gushed in excitement. Accepting the ring and his word for what is was, Shaquita pulled him up where they engaged in another embrace. Law placed kisses on her neck as he led her over towards the couch.

"Wait baby. Make sure the stove off." Shaquita said to him before going inside her pocket and retrieving her vibrating phone.

Noticing it was Monday who was shooting her a text, Shaq slid the bar across to read the text message from her. Surely, she was letting her know that her flight was boarding, or so Shaquita thought until she read the message.

Monday*: Just letting you know that my flight is boarding and that I love you so much.. Thanks for always being in my corner, no matter what, and you were right about Block and me keeping the baby from him.... That's why I decided to get an abortion. Thanks for showing me a good time...and you were right.... THERE'S NOTHING LIKE SUMMERTIME IN THE CHI!*

✺ 28 ✺

he Next Summer

Shaquita searched online for the perfect spot to get her nails done. Coming across an Instagram page belonging to a chick name Lilyana, Shaq fell in love with her work after viewing the first couple of pictures. Going to her bio to book an appointment at Petal's & Pedi's, Shaquita selected the dates her and Law would be in Miami next week and got up from the bed. Exiting out of the bedroom, Shaq made her way down the hall to her daughter's room. Peaking in on Diamond while she slept, she then made her way downstairs to the living room.

"Your mom called while you were sleep. She said she'll be over later to see her grand baby." Law reported from the kitchen while she flopped down on the couch.

"Diamond is only three months and my mom been by to see her every damn day." Shaq replied, shaking her head from side to side.

Her and her mother was able to mend their relationship and after hearing her side of the story, Shaquita understood her mother's decision a little more. Forgiving and moving forward, not only did they fix their relationship but so did Marsha and Marcia. It had been years since the two sat down and spoke but all that changed when Monday went back to California.

"You order the pizza?" Shaquita grabbed the remote control and asked her boyfriend who joined her on the couch.

"Nah I was, but Block said he was finna come over and...." Law paused at the sound of the doorbell.

"And there that nigga go right there." He continued, standing to his feet and answering the door.

Searching for something good to watch on tv while Law answered the front door for his best friend, Shaq settled on a new episode of *Wild n Out* before dropping the remote and springing to her feet when she heard her baby girl cry out. Diamond Dior Bishop had her wrapped around her finger, but she wouldn't have it any other way. Being a mother was the best feeling in the world and she had her daughter to thank for that.

"That's not Diamond crying, Shaquita.... That's Jewel's spoiled ass." Monday walked in behind Block, who carried their two-month-old in her pink and brown car seat.

"And that's why Diamond spoiled too. She's always running whenever she hears her crying." Law followed behind her and said before closing the front door shut.

"Shut the fuck up." Shaq turned to Law and snapped, sticking her middle finger high in the air.

"Come on Monday, you can put Jewel in Diamond's basinet." She instructed, heading up the stairs with her sister in tow.

After Monday text her about getting an abortion, Shaquita told Law, who then told Block. Jumping on the next flight to California, he pulled in front of Monday's parents' house, demanding she talk to him. Confessing his love and her doing the same, Monday packed up what she wanted and moved to Chicago for good. Block being granted custody of his son, who Monday helped raised as well, the couple went from a summer fling to a full-blown family.

"Okay.... Okay.. So, let me see the ring!" Shaquita squealed the moment they entered Diamond's nursery.

Monday grinned from ear to ear before placing her daughter down and showing off her Emerald cut sapphire and pearl oval shaped diamond halo engagement ring. In love with the cut, both girls jumped up and down in excitement.

"I can't believe he remembered the first time seeing you and proposed on that exact day, a year later." Shaquita noted while taking a closer look at the ring.

"Yeah me either……. I love that nigga." Monday replied before the two headed down the stairs to join their men.

It was couple's game night and since Monday had class in the morning, they had to start early. Never in a million years would Shaq have thought that one summer in Chicago would change her life forever and she knew for a fact that Monday felt the same. From starting a new relationship with their father to growing as sisters, that summer was definitely one for the books and if she could, she would….. DO IT ALL OVER AGAIN!

THE MUTHAFUCKN' END

Summertime With A

Chicago- 6/20
Miami- 6/21
Detroit- 6/22
Houston- 6/23
Birmingham- 6/24
Tampa- 6/25
Nashville- 6/26
New York- 6/27
Philly- 6/28
Memphis- 6/29
Atlanta- 6/30

Thug

Text TwylaT to 22828 for releases and exclusives